REPRISAL

DEREK JORDAN

ISBN: 979-8-218-61780-6

Jordan Marked Publishing

900 Washington Street

Middletown, Connecticut 06457

United States

First and foremost, I would like to give a huge shout out to God. Without him, none of this would be possible. And to family, friends, and to those we lost in the physical form.

A huge thank you to my friend and editor, Custodio Gomes, for their keen eye and dedication to making this book the best it could be.

PROLOGUE

The old man felt a warm sense of pride as he stepped out of the bodega, turning to his wife with a grin.

"Baby, I told you today was my day," he chuckled, holding up the winning ticket like it was made of gold.

She laughed, patting his arm.

"Oh, look at you, mister big shot," she teased, eyes bright with shared joy.

They ambled toward the car, both too caught up in their small moment of happiness to notice the two men approaching until it was too late. A fist cracked across the old man's jaw, sending him stumbling back, dazed and confused.

"Please, somebody help us!," his wife cried, voice breaking with terror as one of the attackers grabbed her purse. "Oh Lord, help us!"

Her words went unanswered. The young men moved like shadows, no remorse in their eyes, just the ruthless, quick work of emptying pockets and ripping away anything that looked valuable.

"Shut her up," one of them hissed, delivering a swift kick to the old man's side as he lay gasping on the pavement.

Without hesitation, the second goon punched the frail dark-skinned woman viciously in the face while she pleaded. But before they could share another word, their attackers bolted, disappearing down the street, leaving the couple beaten and broken on the ground.

"Baby, are you alright?" she whispered, her hand reaching out to him, trembling.

The bodega door swung open, and the owner stepped out, eyes widening as he took in the scene.

"Oh my goodness," he muttered, rushing over to the elderly couple.

"Mr. Holt, Mrs. Holt, you alright? What the hell happened!?"

The old woman looked up, eyes filled with tears, clutching her husband's hand.

"They took it all, Tony. They took everything... everything we just won!"

Tony shook his head, his face twisted in frustration and pity.

"Damn animals, hitting on elders like that," he spat, kneeling beside them. Tony was an elderly man himself. He was burning up with anger.

"Ain't no respect out here no more."

Tony glanced around the darkened street, knowing the men were long gone but helpless to change what had just happened. He didn't see it on the camera, but he heard Mrs. Holt's cry for help. He arrived two seconds after the thugs disappeared around the corner.

...

Not a single cloud blemished the sky. Marcel strolled through Fulton Park, Houston trotting by his side—a wiry little Chihuahua that thought he was ten feet tall. The park was alive with the kind of energy Marcel craved but never truly felt. Families lounged on blankets, soaking up the sun, reading books, sipping drinks. Kids dashed around, laughing as they played tag. Old heads sat by the pond, tossing crumbs to the ducks, and other Waterbury folks drifted along with their dogs in tow. A group of teens slung footballs back and forth, stretching into the eighty-degree weather.

But none of it could clear the mental fog choking Marcel's mind. He'd left his Albert Place apartment hoping the sunshine might wash some of it away, but it didn't. Houston needed the walk anyway. Exercise was one of the few things keeping Marcel from slipping entirely into the darkness.

At thirty-five, Marcel had done dirt—killed men who had it coming without flinching. But when it came to taking an innocent life, that hit different. No remorse for laying Ivory down; she played a dirty game and lost. Simple. But his best friend Lupe got killed on his birthday because of her, and that weight stayed heavy. The worst part wasn't even Lupe. It was Asia—her face haunted him every time he closed his eyes. That frozen look on her face when Marcel pulled the trigger lived in his head rent-free.

A year passed, and the streets started talking. Marcel caught wind that Asia wasn't part of the setup. She had been with Ivory that night because she needed a ride home. She didn't know about the hit. Didn't know Ivory and her brothers had plans to rob. She was just caught up in it, like collateral damage. The truth hit Marcel like a freight train. He'd killed an innocent woman. No amount of drinking or fighting could drown out the guilt that ate him alive. Nights got darker, days longer. Every time he closed his eyes, he saw her face. Asia's smile haunted him, a ghost he couldn't escape. He'd been a killer before, but this was different. This wasn't business. This was his mistake, his sin. And he couldn't run from it.

But Asia? She ran. Marcel spent weeks tracking her down, his mind twisted up with betrayal and vengeance. She had been there with Ivory, laughing, sipping drinks, acting like everything was sweet. He couldn't let that slide. When he finally found her in a run-down motel off the interstate, it was late, and she was asleep next to a sleeping man he didn't recognize. Marcel didn't hesitate. He crept in quiet. She didn't even wake up when he pressed the pillow to her face. The shot was muffled since he added a silencer, but it was final. He left her there, lifeless, and walked out without looking back.

Ivory and her two worthless brothers were the only ones who deserved those bullets. But Big Jake—a burly, light-skinned cat from the strip club where Marcel and Lupe met Ivory—had tipped him off. It was a setup. Asia just happened to be in the wrong place, caught up with the wrong crowd, but she didn't know what was really going down. Marcel didn't find that out until after the fact, and Big Jake's words echoed in his mind on a loop ever since.

Now, a mile into the walk, Marcel found himself playing fetch with Houston. That's when she appeared—a Chocolate Lab tugging a leash and dragging along a woman who could've stepped off a magazine cover. She was tall, with smooth brown skin, curves that filled out a sky-blue sundress, and Bohemian braids that slid over her shoulder like silk, the ends brushing against the curve of her chest.

She looked like K.J. Smith from "Sistas." Marcel had seen her before but never worked up the nerve to speak. He wasn't ugly—slim, dark-skinned, built from years of grinding—but she had that kind of beauty that made him second-guess himself.

The Lab yanked its leash, pulling her closer. Houston ran ahead, wagging his tail, and the two dogs circled each other, sniffing. Marcel smirked as Houston nosed the Lab's backside, and the bigger dog didn't even flinch.

Her laugh was soft, almost melodic. "He's adorable! What's his name? And you trust him without a leash?"

Marcel grinned. "Houston. And yeah, it takes training. But if you're consistent, dogs can pick up just as much as people—within reason, of course."

She shook her head, watching as the Lab tried to tug her off course again. "I swear, I think Dixie walks me, not the other way around."

Marcel squatted down, eye-level with Dixie. Houston gave a quick bark, but Marcel calmed him with a subtle hand gesture. Dixie sniffed his fingers, then rolled over, belly up, inviting a rub. Marcel obliged, running his hands along the Lab's stomach, feeling the dog relax under his touch.

The woman's eyes widened in surprise.

"Wow. She never does that for anyone but me and my daughter. What's your secret?"

"Nothing special," Marcel shrugged. "Dogs pick up on vibes."

She laughed, her eyes warm and inviting.

"Well, your vibe must be one of a kind. Dixie's never trusted anyone this quick. I don't even know your name, and here you are giving her belly rubs."

Marcel stood, brushing dirt off his knees, and extended his hand. "Marcel."

"Nyomi."

They shook hands, and the touch lingered a moment longer than necessary. As they talked, Marcel learned Nyomi had just finished her APRN program, ready to start fresh somewhere else. Her daughter was about to graduate high school, and Nyomi was planning their escape from Waterbury. College was on the horizon, and she wanted a new life for them both.

Marcel listened, smiling at her jokes and easy laughter, but his mind stayed restless. She had no idea about the demons chewing at his insides. When she mentioned an abused puppy, his focus sharpened instantly.

"This person live near you?" Marcel asked, his tone casual.

Nyomi gave him a cautious look. "Not really close, no. But sometimes you have to pick your battles, you know? It kills me to think about that poor puppy, though."

Marcel's jaw tightened. "Where's the pup?"

"You're serious, aren't you?" she asked, studying him.

"Yeah. You want the puppy safe, right?"

Nyomi sighed, glancing around the park before answering. "It's on Dikeman Street. But the people in that house... they're dangerous. I think they're cooking something in there—maybe fentanyl. My cousin's husband is a cop so I'm in the loop with that kind of stuff."

Marcel nodded, already knowing the spot she was talking about. He used to run streets in many cities himself, before fentanyl became the new devil in town. He didn't mess with it, though—too many people ended up six feet deep. He was trying to leave that life behind, but some things wouldn't let him go. His conscience was still holding court over all the dirt he'd done.

"So... where exactly?" he pressed.

"Dikeman Street," she repeated.

Silence fell between them. Marcel shifted gears.

"You come here often?"

"Yeah," Nyomi said with a small smile. "But once my daughter graduates, we're out of here. Waterbury isn't what I expected it to be."

Marcel chuckled. "Where you from originally?"

"The Bronx."

Marcel laughed again. "And you thought Waterbury was gonna be better?"

"I had hopes," she said with a playful smirk, glancing at her watch phone. "Sorry, I've gotta run. My daughter's waiting for me."

Marcel, a man who feared no one and killed with his bare hands, suddenly felt shy.

"Uh... Can I, uh... reach you sometime?"

Nyomi gave him a teasing grin. "As long as you're not a creep or a criminal."

Marcel laughed nervously as she handed him her phone. While he punched in his number, the guilt over Asia crept back in, taunting him like a ghost. He shoved the thought aside, gave Nyomi her phone, and grinned.

"Why not send me your number?" she asked, amused.

"Because I'm not a creep," Marcel replied with a sly grin.

They shared a quick laugh before Nyomi waved good-bye, leading Dixie away.

That night, Marcel sat on the porch of the three-family house on Albert Place, his surrogate father Buddy's spot.

The air smelled of street grime and burnt rubber, and the buildings leaned too close together. He lit a joint, taking in the familiar chaos of the neighborhood, and exhaled slowly. His mind spun with thoughts of Dikeman Street.

Robbing and shutting down that trap house was already on his radar. The puppy was just a bonus.

1

LOVELOCK, NEVADA

The desert didn't care if you lived or died. The heat sat heavy, thick like a blanket, suffocating any breeze before it could even try to blow through the sand and rocks. Cactus and mesquite bushes stood scattered across the land, quiet witnesses to the endless cycle of predator and prey. The night air was alive with the sounds of creatures hunting and being hunted.

Richard Hahns loved every bit of it. He wasn't just from Nevada; the desert was his home, his sanctuary, and his playground. At thirty-nine, he'd never left the state—not even once—and he didn't need to. Everything he wanted, everything he needed, was right here. He knew the desert better than most men knew their wives, and he knew exactly where people buried their secrets. Bodies were just another part of the landscape to him, as long as they didn't get in his way.

Richard was built stocky and mean, with a shock of wild red curls stuffed under a greasy New York Mets hat. His dirty white tank top clung to his sweaty frame, and black windbreakers sagged on his hips. A tangled mass of beard covered most of his face, hiding the rotting teeth beneath. His mouth was a disaster—his front two teeth long gone, the rest blackened with plaque—but he smiled anyway, a wicked grin full of menace.

The nineteen-year-old Mexican girl beneath him didn't have a chance. Her limbs went limp, her breath cut off as he tightened his grip around her throat. Richard's hips moved in a slow, deliberate rhythm, even as her life slipped away, her face turning blue and her eyes going dull. He didn't stop—not when she was gone, not until he was done. When he finally finished, he sat back, catching his breath, the grin never leaving his face.

With her lifeless body still warm in the bed of his truck, Richard grabbed a shovel and got to work. The hole had to be deep—deep enough that no coyote or curious hiker would find her. He shoveled until his back ached and the sun peeked over the horizon, promising another scorching day. Once the girl was buried, he wiped the sweat from his brow and tossed the shovel into the back of his truck.

As he drove away, the desert stretched endlessly before him, silent and uncaring. He promised himself—again—that this would be the last time. No more choking. No more cutting. No more killing. But promises meant nothing to Richard Hahns. They never did.

2

WATERBURY, CONNECTICUT

The moon hung low over the city, glowing like a rusty coin. Willow Street was alive, buzzing with the usual suspects—dealers, junkies, nosy neighbors, and hustlers watching every move. A police cruiser sat crooked at the intersection, its lights off, forgotten after blocking traffic for hours. Now the flow was back to normal, just another night in Waterbury.

A dead body, another casualty of fentanyl, had just been zipped into a body bag and loaded into the coroner's van. It was routine now, nothing new.

Officers Hayden Oates and Reginald Sharpe made their way through the alley, stepping over trash and rats scurrying through leaking garbage bags. The stink hit them in waves—puke, piss, and something else, something foul that clung to the air. A dumpster nearby dripped with a thick, greasy liquid that neither of them wanted to identify. Both men wore the same grimace, trying not to breathe too deep.

Hayden slid into the passenger seat and exhaled hard. He was only twenty-eight, fresh out of the academy, and tonight's shift had taken a toll on him. Seeing a young Black kid rotting in an alley was different than anything he'd expected when he first put on the badge. It made the job feel heavy, like a weight he couldn't shake.

Reggie, on the other hand, carried himself like he was made of Teflon. The dead kid didn't faze him one bit. It was just another body to him, and his careless attitude grated on Hayden's nerves.

"I'm starving," Reggie muttered, already thinking about food. "Let's get out of this dump before another one of these zombies hits the ground."

Six months. Six long months of keeping his mouth shut, waiting until his probation was over so he could finally stand up to Reggie. Hayden had reached his limit tonight. If the dead kid had been white, Reggie would have been playing nice, talking to the parents, maybe even shedding a tear. But this was a Black kid, and Reggie didn't care.

"That zombie," Hayden said quietly, "was Black."

Reggie's face twisted into a sneer, his wide nose flaring in annoyance.

"So am I. What's your point?"

"No point," Hayden shot back, his tone cold. "Just saying some respect wouldn't hurt."

They stopped walking, standing face-to-face in the alley. Reggie looked at Hayden like his brain slipped out of his head.

"You got off probation and now you wanna play Malcolm X? Don't pull that Medgar Evers shit with me, rookie."

Hayden didn't flinch. He met Reggie's glare head-on, a slow smirk spreading across his face.

"What if I do?"

For a moment, neither man moved. The tension

between them was thick, the kind of thing that could explode with just the right spark. But before things could boil over, the police radio crackled to life, reporting a shooting two blocks away.

Without a word, they both turned toward the car. Reggie muttered something under his breath, but he kept his mouth shut after that. Hayden had surprised him—stood his ground when Reggie least expected it.

The drive to the next crime scene was silent, the air between them heavy with unspoken tension.

...

The Hyatt ballroom gleamed with polished floors and crystal chandeliers, a glittering cage for the carefully curated crowd sipping champagne and nodding on cue. The host, a tall woman in a navy-blue gown, tapped the mic, her lips stretching into a professional smile.

"Ladies and gentlemen," she began, her voice smooth, "it is my distinct honor to present this year's National Social Worker of the Year Award to someone whose tireless dedication has transformed lives. Please welcome Christina Haynes."

The applause rolled in, measured and polite, as Christina Haynes rose from her table. Her navy dress shimmered under the spotlights, the same color as the hosts, like they had shopped from the same catalog. She moved with a calculated grace, every step an echo of self-assuredness. Her smile stretched wide, a porcelain mask that hid everything but what the crowd wanted to see.

From her table, a group of colleagues cheered, their faces glowing with pride—or maybe the free wine. On stage, Christina accepted the crystal trophy, her fingers brushing over its surface like she was admiring her own reflection. She stood before the mic, pausing for effect as the crowd settled.

"Thank you," she began, her voice smooth, practiced. "This award is not just a recognition of my work but a testament to the resilience of those we serve."

Her words landed like a politician's promise, vague and unchallengeable. The audience nodded along, faces glazed with admiration. Christina played the room like a master conductor, her voice rising and falling in perfect rhythm.

"To my incredible team," she continued, "your unwavering dedication inspires me every day. And to the families we've had the privilege to assist—your courage is the reason we do this work."

The applause broke out again, but Christina held up a hand, signaling she wasn't done. Her eyes scanned the room, locking with the host, the committee members, the donors, every face that mattered.

"Finally, I want to thank my mentor, John Frampton," she said, her voice dipping into an almost reverent tone. "He taught me that real change begins with empathy and a relentless pursuit of justice."

"This award," she finished, "is proof that together, we can build a more just and compassionate world."

The applause swelled, louder this time, and Christina soaked it in. She stepped back from the podium, her smile unwavering as she returned to her table. Colleagues swarmed her, showering her with praise and hugs, their voices blurring into a meaningless buzz.

3

Katia Musa flicked the tilt wand on the dirty blinds, letting in the blazing heat of the Carlin, Nevada sun. The dull light washed over the cramped apartment on Bowean Lane, giving everything an even grittier edge. Sleep wasn't an option for Katia. The air inside was thick and dead, no air conditioning to break the suffocating heat. Candice, her housemate, sprawled naked on the couch, her blonde hair matted against her flushed face. She was still knocked out from a cocaine bender and a long night of sex with Sloan. The sunlight creeping in only made Candice shift and grunt before falling back into her drugged-out sleep.

In the bathroom, Katia stared at her reflection, her body rigid with pain and anger. A single tear slipped from her piercing hazel eyes. Her mocha-colored skin gleamed under the harsh fluorescent light, but she barely noticed. Life had torn her apart, stripping her of her dignity, her future, her identity. Twenty-one and trapped in hell, she was just another pawn in Sloan's sex-trafficking operation. Her father was Nigerian, her mother Puerto Rican, and somewhere in her bloodline was a deep strength. That strength was all that kept her from breaking completely. She didn't have a drug problem like the rest. The pictures Sloan showed her of her mother, father, and a few relatives was all she needed to see to stay put in Nevada.

She traced a finger along her body, her hand pausing at a scar on her side. It was from a "john" who had gone wild a year ago, a wound that served as a reminder of the world she was placed in. The mental pain never left her. The same went for the hands and mouths that had claimed her without consent. The memories left her paralyzed with disgust and rage. Curtis, the man she had once trusted, had led her into this life. She wanted him dead.

Angel Ramos barged in, her face tight with worry. Angel wasn't much taller than a teenager, her curvy frame wrapped in tight jeans and a tank top. Her long brown hair clung to her damp neck. Kansas City was where she was from, but that life might as well have been a dream. Now, she was just another broken piece in Sloan's stable.

"Where's Hazel? She didn't come in last night?" Angel's voice was sharp, cutting through Katia's thoughts. Katia shook her head.

"She didn't come back. What's going on?" Her voice sounded flat even to herself.

Angel's face darkened. "Hazel's been gone two days. Two. Lulu sent her out there without grooming her, nothing. She's always about money, but if she's so damn hungry, she should be out there herself, not putting Hazel on the block like that."

Angel's hands balled into fists.

"And with this serial killer out here? Hazel's gone."

Angel stormed over to the couch and shook Candice

awake. The blonde groaned, pulling herself into a sitting position.

"What?" she mumbled, rubbing her eyes.

"You see Hazel last night?" Angel pressed, her tone sharper now. Candice frowned.

"I saw her yesterday morning, before Lulu sent her out. Or maybe the day before. What's the big deal?"

Angel slumped onto the same sofa Katia slept on and lit a joint she pulled from her cleavage. She exhaled a cloud of smoke, her face twisted with frustration.

"Hazel didn't come back. Lulu sent her out there raw, and now she's gone. Just like Toya. Just like Sherry, Renee, Arlene. Nobody cares. Nobody's looking for them. They just bring in more girls like it's nothing. I'm so sick of this shit!"

The room fell silent except for the distant hum of traffic outside. Candice, feeling untouchable under Sloan's protection, leaned back, unconcerned. Angel's eyes were heavy with despair, the anger in her voice fading into a cold, resigned quiet. Katia's thoughts drifted as she watched Angel take another drag. This wasn't living. This was dying slowly. Every day, another girl disappeared. Every day, Sloan's grip on their lives tightened. Katia clenched her fists, her nails biting into her palms. She wasn't going to end up like the others. If she had to burn everything to the ground to escape, then so be it. The cost didn't matter anymore. Freedom was the only thing left to fight for.

4

Nate Lane stepped into the cramped bathroom, the air thick with mildew and grime from fixtures long past their prime. The funky shower curtain, smeared with soap scum and dirt, clung to the sides of the tub. He popped open the chipped medicine cabinet, tossing back the beat-up tube of toothpaste, then leaned in close to the cracked mirror. The jagged fracture ran like a scar down the center, splitting his reflection in two. Nate didn't mind; he'd been looking in this same busted mirror since he was a kid. It still got the job done.

He tilted his head, checking his fresh lineup one more time. His hairline and pencil-thin mustache were edged sharp—tight work from the straight razor he'd taught himself to use, practicing on his own until he got it perfect. Nate always kept himself clean. Even when things around him were falling apart, his grooming stayed on point.

At six feet tall and built like a linebacker, the maroon button-up shirt he squeezed into was snug across his chest. His khakis weren't faring any better, cutting into his waist. But they were the best he had, and there wasn't money for anything else. He needed a job bad—new threads, bills paid, and most importantly, to help his mother, Betty. She was riding that dope hard and hadn't been the same since the accident that put her in a wheelchair ten years back. Nate, just eighteen and fresh out of high school, knew the streets weren't waiting on him, but he was ready to get out there and make it happen.

Only thing was, Floyd—his big brother—had gone ghost. And that hit Nate harder than he ever let on. Floyd was his rock, the one person Nate thought would always be solid. Last Nate saw him, he'd walked his brother to the commuter lot, chilled with him until that bus rolled out. Floyd was fresh off a work-release program, hyped about a new construction job in Nevada. It was supposed to be a clean slate for him, a fresh start far from the drama they grew up in. But since that day? Nothing. No call, no text. Just static.

From the bathroom, Nate hollered through the door.

"Ma! You straight?"

He knew she wasn't straight. She'd been spiraling deeper into that crack pipe ever since their pops skipped town. Nate and Floyd had tried their best to hold it down for her, cooking meals, cleaning the house, taking care of her meds, but it was never enough. The addiction had claws in her soul. Still, that was their mother—she did what she could when they were little, even if "what she could" wasn't much.

Her voice drifted through the door, scratchy and slow.

"Nate, you going on 'bout these jobs again?"

Nate smirked, combing his waves in the mirror.

"I ain't settling for just any bullshit, Ma. My generation—we ain't about to kill ourselves working for pennies. I'm trying to build something real."

"I don't wanna hear none of that!" she snapped. "Your brother is trying to build something real. He was in prison, got to the halfway house, and went west even though we haven't heard from him."

Nate didn't miss the flash of hurt in his mother's eyes. She felt something was wrong.

He shook his head, still brushing his hair.

"Y'all Gen X always riding us. But give us some time— we gon' change this whole system. Watch. We aiming for real healthcare, longer lifespans. You'll see."

There was no reply from Betty this time. Nate figured she'd nodded off mid-argument, like she always did when the drugs weighed her down too heavy. He chuckled to himself, tossing the comb on the sink.

"Damn, Ma. You lucky you got me. You know I could talk you to sleep all day."

When she still didn't answer, a chill ran down Nate's spine. He stepped out the bathroom, scanning the cluttered living room. The TV was on, blaring the news nobody paid attention to. The walls were stained yellow from cigarette smoke, and old pictures of him and Floyd were scattered across the place. The sectional couch they'd hauled from Bunker Hill with an old friend years ago was now buried under a mess of clothes.

"Ma?" His voice dropped a notch, something uneasy settling in his gut.

She was slumped in her wheelchair by the wicker table, head dipped low into her chest. Foam bubbled from the corner of her mouth, spilling onto the Nike logo on her faded green sweatshirt.

"Ma!" Nate shouted, rushing to her side. He shook her shoulder, but her body was heavy—lifeless. There was no movement, no breath. Just the eerie stillness of death.

"Come on, Ma... Please! Wake up!" His voice cracked as panic gripped him tight.

He crouched down, pressing his forehead against hers, praying for any sign she might still be there. But there was nothing. No heartbeat. No shallow breaths. Just cold silence. The foam around her mouth confirmed what he already feared—she was gone, lost to the drugs that had been slowly stealing her away for years.

Nate crumbled, hugging her lifeless body tight, his tears soaking into her sweatshirt.

"Ma... No... No... Please!" He rocked her back and forth, begging the universe to reverse time, to let him have just one more moment with her.

When his sobs slowed, and the weight of reality set in, Nate pulled out his phone, dialing his friend who lived upstairs and 911 with trembling fingers. But after he made the calls, he didn't move. He sat there on the floor, still holding her, still whispering, still hoping—until the first responders came and tore her from his arms.

And just like that, the last piece of Nate's world crumbled.

5

Buddy "Charles" Turner sat back in his old brown recliner, readers perched low on his nose, scanning the pages of his will. For thirty-five years, he'd been on the run, a ghost to the law. To Buddy, life insurance was just bait for the feds. Now, though, cancer was gunning for him, creeping through his pancreas and letting him know the clock was ticking. A month ago, the doctor laid it out plain, and Buddy knew it was only a matter of time before the lights went out. He had one more thing to square away before the end—tell Marcel, the kid he raised like his own blood.

After taking a piss that looked more like red Kool-Aid than urine, Buddy stared at the bloody water swirl down the bowl. He shuffled over to the mirror and studied his reflection. Gray hair circled the edges of his head like a halo, the top bald as a baby's ass, and his beard was thick and snowy white. Buddy cracked a small smile—felt like peace was finally sneaking up on him. He was tired. Tired of running, tired of the life, and ready to punch his ticket to the other side. God had a spot saved for him, that much Buddy believed.

But the one thing sitting heavy on him was Marcel. The boy was a loose cannon, and if Buddy checked out without setting things straight, Marcel's head might go all the way off the rails. As if summoned by Buddy's thoughts, Marcel's heavy footsteps echoed in the living room. Buddy cut on the water at the sink, buying himself a moment, exhaling hard like the weight of the conversation ahead was a thousand pounds.

Buddy shuffled into the living room, lowering himself into his recliner with a grunt. Marcel was lounging on the couch, absently playing with Houston, the little mutt they took in a couple years back.

"How's it feel outside?" Buddy asked, scratching his beard.

Marcel set the dog on the floor and shrugged. "Hot."

Buddy's mind raced, weighing whether this was the right time. Marcel's vibe felt off—darker than usual. But there was no dodging this conversation. He had to rip the Band-Aid off.

"You got a minute?" Buddy asked, voice low.

Marcel stretched, leaning back like he had all the time in the world. "I got plenty, Pop. What's up?"

"I'm dyin'."

Buddy let the words drop like bricks—no frills, no tears, just the cold facts.

Marcel blinked, confusion clouding his face.

"What you mean?"

"Exactly what it sound like."

The room grew heavy with silence, thick enough to choke on. Marcel stared at Buddy like he was trying to decode the meaning, searching his face for a punchline that never came.

"How?" Marcel finally asked, voice tight.

"Pancreatic cancer."

Another beat of silence stretched between them, a canyon neither wanted to cross.

"How long you known?" Marcel's voice sharpened, cutting through the quiet.

Buddy's gaze drifted off, dodging the question for a moment before he gave it to him straight. "Little over a month."

Marcel sat up, rage flickering in his eyes. "A month?! You knew a whole month and just now telling me?"

Marcel's eyes scanned Buddy's face, and for the first time, he noticed the sickly yellow tint staining Buddy's eyes like faded old paper. How the hell had he missed that? His thoughts raced, all jumbled, like his brain was fighting itself. That's when his phone buzzed on the coffee table.

The vibration rattled the glass surface, then it stopped. Buzzed again. Marcel ignored it, trying to stay locked in on Buddy. But the phone wouldn't quit. It buzzed again, louder this time, demanding his attention.

Frustrated, Marcel snatched it off the table. "He...hello?" he answered, voice shaky.

Whatever was said on the other end hit him like a sledgehammer to the gut. Marcel's friend Nate was on the phone.

Marcel twisted, eyes wide with disbelief.

"What?!" Buddy shouted, the word coming out cracked and sharp.

Buddy watched him, reading Marcel's face like a newspaper headline. Bad news didn't need translation—it was clear as day in the way Marcel's shoulders sagged, the way his jaw clenched tight enough to snap a tooth.

"I'll be right there," Marcel barked into the phone, then slapped it down, already lacing up his sneakers in a frenzy.

He shot a quick, wild glance at Buddy, eyes glossed with panic. "Nate said Betty dead."

6

"Her ass is fat, and she got some big-ass titties. If I was you, I'd be trying to smash," Holland said, taking a heavy swig from the Henny bottle they passed between them. The liquor burned his throat, but he welcomed it. It was Saturday, one-thirty in the morning, and the streets were still theirs to roam. Holland gripped the wheel of a beat-up tan Toyota Camry, pushing it faster than Tuff liked, his hands jittery from the mix of adrenaline and liquor. He flicked a burnt-out Newport out the window into the warm night. The car was borrowed from a crack-head who needed a quick fix. The piece of junk already sputtered twice since they got behind the wheel, and Tuff wasn't trying to get stranded in this heap.

"Slow this piece of shit down, man. I'm not dying in this junk bucket," Tuff grumbled, shifting uneasily in the passenger seat. Holland sucked his teeth and rolled his eyes.

"I'm only hitting forty."

Tuff shot him a hard glare.

"Yeah, well, this ain't our whip, we got a gun under the

seat, and we're sitting on a brick of fent. Popo's out here lurking. One bad move, and we're done."

Holland wasn't exactly a genius, but he knew when to fall back. Fresh out of prison for barely two weeks, and here he was-already dipping his toes into the same muddy waters. But Tuff had a point. Cops were swarming the streets, and if they got caught slipping, it wouldn't be just another night behind bars-it'd be the end.

The two prowled Waterbury's grimy streets like hungry wolves. Hood predators with no loyalty, no code, and no direction. They had robbed four unlucky fools already, and the thrill of it had them on a high. But that brick of fentanyl? That was the real jackpot. And with the clubs about to let out, they figured it was time for one last come-up. Tuff scanned the block with the cold precision of a killer, his beady eyes searching for prey. His heart raced when he spotted a potential mark walking up Walton Street, cradling a duffle bag tight under his arm.

"Bust this right," Tuff muttered, pulling a rubber band from his pocket and tying his dreads into a bun. He yanked his hoodie up, shading his eyes.

"This nigga look ripe."

Holland gave a slow nod, licking his lips.

"Yeah ... Yeah, let's shake this nigga down and call it a night."

They rolled past the mark, dipped right off Walton, and swung up Walnut. Holland killed the headlights and parked behind a red Chevy, just out of sight. They slid out of the Camry like shadows, ready to pounce.

...

A week had passed since Buddy's revelation of death

and Betty's fatal overdose. Nate's living arrangement had changed abruptly. Buddy and Marcel extended their home to the heartbroken young man but couldn't do anything else for him besides being a genuine support system. Marcel and Buddy gave the kid his space, fed him, and provided him with an air mattress. To add more insult to injury, Nate's brother Floyd had no idea that his mother had passed, and Marcel found that disturbing. Unbeknownst to Nate, Marcel had a feeling Floyd was dead.

The streets whispered. He could feel it: the stick-up kids were out there. He'd been watching Holland and Tuff for a minute now. They were on borrowed time. When Marcel saw the security footage of them stomping the Holts and taking all their winnings from the numbers, his blood boiled. Robbing drug dealers? That was business. But beating on old folks? That was some next-level foul shit, and in Marcel's book, that deserved consequences. And Marcel was the consequence.

Marcel watched the street from the second-story window of an abandoned three family home, his binoculars pressed tight against his face. His body was loose from a few shots of whiskey, but his mind was sharp. He needed it to be. The whiskey wasn't for celebration; it was a distraction, a weak attempt to dull the sting of the news he'd gotten earlier that week. Buddy, the man who made him who he was, had pancreatic cancer. The words rang in his head like an unwelcome echo. On top of that, he'd been drowning in memories of Lupe and the stripper, mistakes he couldn't take back, no matter how hard he tried. And tonight, hunting felt like the only thing that made sense.

. . .

He laced up his Sauconys, slid his blade into his waistband, and grabbed a Glock from the stash box by the door. Tonight wasn't about redemption-it was about balance. He saw them now, lurking behind a red Chevy like stray dogs. Marcel took a deep breath and started toward the block. His steps were deliberate, his heartbeat steady as he closed the distance.

"Run that shit!" Tuff's voice cracked like thunder as he jammed the Glock against Marcel's jaw.

Marcel froze, his hands raised high. His dark eyes, calm and steady, locked onto Tuft's jittery hands. Holland snatched the bag from Marcel's shoulder, grinning like he'd won the lottery.

"Yo, this nigga ain't got nothin' but some binoculars!" Holland barked, shaking the bag.

Tuff shifted his stance, his finger dangerously close to the trigger. That's all Marcel needed.

Like lightning, Marcel grabbed Tuff's wrist, twisting it hard until the Glock dropped. Before Holland could react, Marcel had the gun in his own hands. Tuff's face turned pale as Marcel leveled the weapon at his head.

"Come on, dawg!" Holland stammered, backing up. "We just tryin' to eat, man!"

Marcel's voice was ice.

"So were the Holts, and you beat them half to death. This ain't about eatin'. This about you thinkin' you untouchable."

Before Tuff could beg, Marcel pulled the trigger. The gunshot echoed through the street as Tuff's body dropped like a bag of bricks.

Holland froze, his eyes wide with terror. Marcel turned the gun on him.

"Yo, please, man! I got kids!"

Marcel's lip curled.

"So do they...and grandkids."

The second shot was louder than the first. Holland's body hit the pavement, blood pooling around his head. Marcel crouched, wiping the Glock clean before slipping it into Tuft's lifeless hand. He snatched the duffle bag and disappeared into the night, his footsteps silent. The streets were quiet again, but the ghosts of Walton would linger.

7

Barry Huggins' pad sat pretty in Greenwich, one of the swankiest cities in Connecticut. His mansion was walled off, with smooth green lawns, hedges trimmed with precision, and a gate that screamed private only. There was a whole security setup on the grounds, like he was some A-list celeb or politician. His spot had rooftop lounges, patios, balconies—every spot dripped luxury. Inside, the walls flexed with original pieces from Picasso to Van Gogh. Out back, it looked like Tiger Woods could run a whole tournament on the sprawling green lawn. His mansion had everything—bars, a game room, a custom-built basketball court, and a massive kitchen shining with stainless steel everything.

Barry knew how to keep low-key even though his money was loud. He wasn't just pushing weight; he ran numbers too, posing as a legit accountant. To the IRS, Barry was just a guy crunching tax forms, but on the streets? He was that guy moving kilos. He started in Waterbury back in high school, slinging dime bags. By the time he hit George-town, the campus was his playground for weed, coke, and pills. Dean's List four years running, but the real paper came from taxing fiends. His nights were spent counting stacks, setting examples, and ordering hits, all with the same focus he brought to his daytime business meetings.

Kenny G's *Japan* floated from the waterproof Bluetooth speaker as Barry swam his tenth lap in the pool. His chiseled, dark-skinned frame glistened under the early morning sun, water dripping from his bleached high top. Only two years out of Georgetown, and Barry had already made millions from tax fraud, writing false returns, and doctoring books for rich clients who had no idea he was flipping their dough into a fentanyl empire.

He slid out of the water and grabbed a towel, drying off under the burning sun. A thick, brown-skinned woman stood behind the poolside bar, her freshly implanted ass popping in the morning light. Her long, flat-ironed Malaysian weave flowed down her back as she mixed him a Mimosa. Barry's eyes drank her in, his tongue sliding across his lips like a wolf ready to feast.

The woman handed him the Mimosa and perched herself on his lap, her heavy chest pressing against him. She traced his beard, leaning in to kiss him, but Barry turned his cheek, giving her the cold shoulder. His indifference didn't stop her, though—soon, her lips were wrapped around his dick, and he closed his eyes, lost in the moment, until—

"Ahem"

Barry's butler, Cyrus, a stiff old dude with seventy years behind him, cleared his throat. Barry shot him a deadly glance—interruptions didn't fly with him. Workers in the past had paid with broken limbs for getting in his way, and one unlucky bastard bled out for crossing him at the wrong time.

Then Barry remembered. He'd told Dwight to come

through to talk shop. He tapped the woman on the shoulder, signaling her to stop, and dismissed her with a flick of his hand.

"Dwight?"

"Yes, sir."

Barry nodded. "Bring him back here."

Dwight Carr slid into the backyard, his bald head gleaming in the sunlight. His light skin looked pale, and a permanent snarl twisted his crooked lips. His eyes were bloodshot and mean, and his patchy beard only added to his gruff appearance. The gods gave Dwight a bad deal in the looks department, but his mind was razor-sharp. He held a master's degree in international affairs and was Barry's right-hand man. Despite having the brains to go legit, Dwight would unload a clip without hesitation, proving that education didn't cancel out street instincts.

Barry leaned back in his chair, waving Tabitha, the woman from earlier, over.

"Tabitha, another round. D, you good?"

Dwight shook his head, though his gaze lingered on her curves as she sashayed back to the bar.

"We got the plug," Barry said, swirling his drink. "But we need to figure out some new routes. Fentanyl ain't like the other shit."

Dwight sucked his teeth and shook his head.

"We might need a whole new game plan. Ever since we started pushing this shit, the body count jumped."

Barry laughed, deep and slow.

"Come on, D. Ain't nobody trippin' over three junkies. Some more might OD, but that don't stop the money train. Death ain't no deterrent to an addict."

Dwight lit a cigarette and took a slow drag, blowing the smoke through his nose.

"That's the difference between me and you. I know it only takes one wrong death. A politician's kid OD? Or some clean-cut college kid? They gonna be on us, hard."

Barry scratched his beard, knowing Dwight had a point. But the rush of cash was too sweet to ignore. Moving fentanyl had bumped Barry's income into another tax bracket, but with several bodies dropping this week alone, even Barry knew things were getting messy.

"I hear you, D. I do," Barry said. "But right now, demand is stupid high, and the supply feels endless. I'm not cutting the faucet over a couple of old heads kicking the bucket. Hell, their deaths are free promo. It's fixable."

Dwight shook his head. "Fixable? How?"

Barry leaned forward, his smile sly and dangerous. "Diego."

Dwight blinked, confused. "Diego? That little dude from Park Ave? What's he got to do with anything?"

Barry grinned wider. "Yeah, that Diego. I know he's young, just got here from Mexico a few weeks ago. But you gotta stop thinking so damn small, D."

Dwight chuckled, shaking his head as he flicked ash from his cigarette.

"Alright, educate me."

"This kid used to cook fentanyl with his uncles in an outdoor lab down in Mexico. He's a chemist in the making. No one around here can whip this shit without killing themselves in the process."

Dwight shook his head, still doubtful. "So what's your angle?"

Barry leaned back in his chair; eyes gleaming with ambition.

"I'm gonna make Diego an offer he can't refuse. Big

money, long-term deals-and some fine print he won't notice 'til it's too late."

Dwight laughed, nodding. "A'ight, say no more."

They kicked around more ideas, strategizing like generals plotting a war. The conversation flowed smoothly until Dwight checked his watch, realizing he needed to bounce. But just as he stood up, a thought hit him.

"Oh yeah, Holland and Tuff got smoked last night."

Barry's eyes narrowed.

"That makes six."

"Seven," Dwight corrected, his voice low.

The two men shared a heavy silence, the weight of uncertainty settling between them. They didn't want to admit it out loud, but something was happening in the streets-something neither of them could control. Dealers, killers, and gangsters were getting dropped left and right, and Barry had a hunch that some rogue cop might be behind it all. Barry finally broke the silence.

"Tell our boys on the corners to keep their heads on a swivel. Eyes open. I don't want nobody gettin' caught slippin'."

Dwight nodded, adjusting his jacket.

"Bet. I'll make sure they know what time it is."

The two men exchanged a firm handshake before heading back inside the mansion, both knowing the storm was coming-whether they were ready for it or not.

8

The sky bled deep purple, the kind of dusk that carried heat long after the sun dipped, wrapping everything in a sticky, muggy film. It wasn't the scorching one-thirteen it hit earlier, but it was still heavy, thick enough to make a man feel trapped in his own skin. Crickets, frogs, and all kinds of bugs buzzed and screamed into the night, filling the air with a noise that only made the silence louder. Sloan sat back in the ride, his mind on money. Five years back, some fool hired a construction crew to build a gas station, diner, and a casino in the desert. But the job fell through when the owner's pockets went dry, leaving behind nothing but half-built skeletons scattered in the dirt. Where most folks saw a ghost town, Sloan saw potential -potential for a whole lot of sin. When it came to chasing dollars, Sloan had a gift. He didn't just own real estate -he owned people. Boys, girls, men, women, and even forty folks who didn't fit into any box. He played the streets like a game of chess, moving pieces to stack cash. Human trafficking, drugs, murder-Sloan's hustle was limitless. In fifteen years, he'd made more than most men could dream of. If his game was legal, he'd be in the highest tax bracket. But for Sloan, it was never about that. It was about power, control -using people like currency to keep his empire fat.

Gus, an Albanian man as well as Sloan's driver, rolled through the abandoned lot, easing the ride over stacks of lumber and past plastic tarps flapping in the breeze. Tractors sat like skeletons, rusting and waiting to be useful again. Sloan cracked his window in the back seat, letting a bit of the night air swirl in as he leaned back in the leather. Whether it was a Range Rover or a Telluride-Sloan didn't care. It was luxury. With a flick of his diamond-studded cigar cutter, he sliced the end of a Padron and sparked it up, filling the car with the sweet, slow burn of high-end tobacco. He exhaled, smoke curling into the night as memories danced in his head. Raised in the gutter with pimps, goons, and drifters, Sloan had learned early to get rich or get the fuck out of dodge. Life had used him up when he was a kid, passing him around like a party favor. So now, he used people the same way, and he was damn good at it. At forty-four, he wore his success like a second skin. Fair-skinned with a slight build, his hair was slicked back into a neat ponytail, and his villain-arched eyebrows gave him a permanent sinister glare. His five-o'clock shadow was razor sharp, and the loud Hawaiian shirts he wore always left his thick chest hair on display. The diamond-studded chain around his neck was somebody's year's salary. Sloan didn't give a fuck about anything, or anyone-empathy was for suckers. Those who knew him called him the Devil's understudy.

Gus eased the car to a crawl, parking in front of the skeletal building Sloan had plans to flip first. Sloan squinted into the night, annoyed.

"They ain't here. What the fuck, Gus? Thought you handled this."

Gus swallowed hard, beads of sweat crawling down his temple. He silently cursed whoever was running late with the human cargo. Sloan was volatile; murder was always one wrong move away. But just as Gus felt his stomach drop, headlights cut through the darkness, and the GMC Savana rolled into the lot.

Inside the van, Malone, a lanky, light-skinned dude, ran his mouth to anyone willing to listen.

"Man, I ain't had no job in five years. Hell yeah, I took this gig. What I look like sayin' no? If I don't come up with this arrearage cash, I'm headin' right back to the joint."

A thick, freckle-faced blonde named Bethany sat across from him, nodding along.

"Looked legit to me. The orientation packet they gave us at the shelter said benefits, room for growth. Sounded like a sweet deal. They said Mississippi at first, but here we are, hoppin' state to state."

Hugo, a short, stocky Puerto Rican, stared out the window, ignoring the chatter. Something wasn't sitting right in his gut. The quiet desert gnawed at him, and every instinct told him to bail. But he kept his mouth shut-fear, real and raw, had its claws in him. It wasn't just fear of the unknown; it was a survival instinct honed from a life of dodging danger. Hugo could smell death lingering close, but saying it out loud felt like inviting it in. Tyrone, an older, dark-skinned brother with a rough beard, leaned back with a grin that made it clear he thought he hit the jackpot.

"Shit, I just got out the joint last month, and now I'm ridin' in a van to some construction gig? Man, life ain't never been this sweet. I did construction before, and I got me some certs, too. I don't care if this gigs in Mississippi or Nevada. Long as the money hit, I'm with it."

Floyd, the youngest of the group, sat tight, muscles tense under his brown skin. His twists, streaked with blond highlights, peeked from under a hoodie. The kid was quiet, but the regret in his eyes spoke loudly. He had that same sixth sense as Hugo, and it told him something wasn't right. But like Hugo, Floyd played it cool waiting, watching, ready to move if things went left.

When the van came to a stop, Sloan and Gus watched as two men stepped out of the front seats. One was a tall, muscle-bound Black man with a clean-shaven, cinnamon-toned face. His partner was an Irish brute, pale with buzzed hair and arms thick like tree stumps.

The Irishman reached for the back door, but before he could grab the handle, Hugo kicked the door open with all his strength. The metal slammed into the Irishman's face with a sick thud, breaking his nose.

"UGHHHHH!"

The Irishman staggered, clutching his face as blood gushed through his fingers. His gun clattered to the ground.

Hugo didn't waste a second. He jumped from the van and sprinted into the desert, desperate for freedom. He made it two hundred feet before the Black man, Trevor, calmly pulled a Glock 19 from his holster. One shot-clean and precise-dropped Hugo with a bullet to the back of the skull, his brains painting the sand.

The van went dead silent, except for the dull thud of Hugo's body hitting the ground. Trevor holstered his piece, eyes cold.

"Anybody else wanna pull some dumb shit? Or y'all ready to introduce yourselves?"

The rest of the group scrambled out of the van. Luz, a

small Latina woman, pissed herself on the spot. Malone stood frozen, mouth hanging open. Bethany buried her face in Floyd's chest, sobbing. Tyrone stayed stone-faced, though his heart pounded in his chest.

Sloan stepped out of the Land Rover and strolled toward the Irishman, who lay groaning, blood seeping between his fingers. The big man managed a grin through the pain-until Sloan drew his pistol.

"Sloan, wait! No, man, no-!"

BOOM.

The gunshot echoed through the lot. The Irishman's grin vanished as blood pooled beneath him, spreading across the ground. Bethany screamed, her voice piercing the night. Sloan walked over, wrapping an arm around her shoulder with a smile so fake it could've been plastic.

"Listen, sweetheart. You got two choices-help me build this little empire I got in mind or end up in ashes. Your call."

He let her go and turned to Trevor. "Clean this mess up. Don't leave no trace."

Trevor watched the taillights of Sloan's Land Rover fade into the distance, wishing for nothing more than a rocket launcher to blow it sky high.

9

The day was already shaping up to be brutal-hot as hell, with some serious grind ahead. Hayden was dragging, wishing the whole thing would be over before it started. The couple living beneath them had been going at it all night. Yelling, stomping, and then fucking like they were the last people on earth. Hayden heard every bit of it. He'd been wide awake since, and it only added to the fire under him to get a house. Living like this was wearing him thin, and Cybil, as always, slept right through the madness.

Hayden grabbed his YETI mug, filled it with coffee, and plopped down at the kitchen table. The radio played low, Urban View filling the room with politics and real talk. Just as he took a sip, Cybil slid up behind him, arms snaking around his shoulders, pulling him close. Hayden inhaled the scent of her-cocoa butter and vanilla-and let himself relax in the moment. She walked around, standing in front of him, her hands in his.

"Good mornin', baby," she whispered with that sing-song sweetness.

"Good mornin', my queen," Hayden replied, pulling her in close and locking lips like they hadn't kissed in years.

Cybil giggled between kisses, her body already responding.

"Hayden, boy, you better stop before we don't leave this house today."

She grinned as her thighs clenched at the thought. But she broke away, just enough to smooth down her navy-blue nursing scrubs. Hayden sat back, watching her with that lazy hunger. Cybil was a sight; her skin a deep, smooth mahogany, tight curls framing her face. Those scrubs hugged her just right, showing off her curves like a promise. They weren't just married; they were in love, for real. That deep, everyday kind of love.

"What they talkin' 'bout this mornin'?" she asked, reaching for her own coffee.

Hayden leaned back.

"Same shit, finance, our voting rights, police bustin' heads."

Cybil rolled her eyes and took a sip.

"They need to talk about the crooked-ass Black cops out here."

Hayden laughed, shaking his head.

"Man, that topics coming'. I get my own personal show every shift, courtesy of that clown-ass nigga."

"They still ain't moved you to another zone?"

"Nah. We too short-staffed. Ain't nobody tryin' to run these streets. That's why I been pickin' up those extra shifts. But not today."

Cybil raised an eyebrow, her lips curving into a slow, teasing grin.

"Oh, you off today, huh? If you told me, I coulda been off too."

Hayden shrugged, a sly smirk pulling at his mouth.

"Ain't too late to call out."

Cybil gave him that look, the one that meant trouble. She pulled her phone from her purse, fingers already working.

"Baby, you don't gotta do that. I can wait till you get back," Hayden said, though his eyes were saying something else. Before Cybil could answer, her iPhone rang, the sound breaking the moment. She answered quick.

"Hey, Mary Anne ... Oh, yeah? That's perfect ... Cool, I'll see you tomorrow."

She hung up, grinning from ear to ear.

"Guess what? They were about to cancel me anyway. Looks like I got the day off, too."

Hayden gave her a look of mock confusion.

"Cancel?"

"Yeah, they got enough nurses today. No need for me to clock in."

Next thing he knew, Cybil's scrubs were in a pile on the floor, and her legs were wrapped tight around his back. Hayden had her pinned to the kitchen counter, delivering slow, deep strokes that had her eyes rolling back. Their moans bounced off the walls, raw and loud, like a payback performance for the noisy neighbors downstairs. They moved like animals, locked in rhythm, and neither one of them cared who heard. And that was just the warm-up.

10

The walls of the roll call room were dressed up in rotary club plaques, a big American flag, and blown-up photos of cops killed on the job—memorials going back thirty years. Officer Reginald Sharpe leaned back in his chair, chopping it up with the other officers, waiting for the shift to kick off. They were talking about George Floyd. Reggie nodded along as Officer Brad Moriarty, a thick-necked, blond buzz-cut ex-Marine with fifteen years on the force, gave his two cents.

"Man, that cop didn't kill him. Floyd killed himself swallowing all that fentanyl. Now the whole damn world's making money off this Black Lives Matter shit," Moriarty grunted, eyes sharp, chest puffed like he meant every word.

"Facts," Reggie chimed in, rolling his eyes. "And now they wanna defund the police? Man, get the fuck outta here with that."

Hayden, who had just poured himself some shitty precinct coffee, shot Reggie a disgusted look but said nothing. Meanwhile, Kurt Cyr, a lanky Irish dude with wild red curls and a scruffy beard, sat across the room listening to

Moriarty and Reggie spit their takes on the matter. He shook his head slow, like they were beyond hope.

"Moriarty, man, this ain't it," Cyr said, leaning forward in his seat. "The way that shit went down? That wasn't just dumb. That was stone-cold cruelty, and now the whole system's cracking under it. You really think the people we're supposed to protect ain't looking at us like murderers in uniform now? That man begged for his life, bro. He—"

"He broke the fuckin' law!" Moriarty snapped, cutting Cyr off. "If he wasn't trying to hustle with a fake twenty, none of this shit woulda happened!"

Reggie jumped in, sipping his cold coffee like it was a shot.

"Bruh, picture us out here, protecting and serving these inbreds with no funding. You think about that, Cyr? What about those rookie cops that went down with Chauvin? You gonna act like their lives don't count? All 'cause George thought a fake twenty was a good idea."

Cyr gave Reggie a look, cold and disgusted, like he'd just scraped him off the bottom of his boot.

"I feel sorry for you, Sharpe," Cyr said with a sneer. "You're a disgrace to your own people, man. A Black man, siding with racist bullshit. That cop snuffed out a man's life like it wasn't shit—like it could've been your brother—and here you are, co-signing that same hate. You're lost, dude. Real talk."

Reggie's eyes shrank into hard little slits.

"Man, fuck you, Cyr!"

The whole room went dead quiet. No captain in sight, just thick tension in the air. Reggie's fists clenched tight, nostrils flaring, as if daring Cyr to say one more word. Cyr just smirked, cocky as ever, and strolled over to sit next to Hayden in the back row like it was nothing.

Reggie stood there fuming, his knuckles white, while his boys backed off, trying to avoid the blow-up. Then the captain strolled in, a stack of folders in hand, looking oblivious to the heat that had just gone down. Roll call kicked off, but Reggie wasn't hearing shit. His eyes drilled into Cyr like he was trying to punch a hole in his skull. All he could think about was how good it'd feel to put a bullet through the side of Cyr's smug face.

After roll call, Reggie stood up, still burning. He caught sight of Hayden shaking Cyr's hand on his way out. That was the final slap in the face. Reggie just stood there, stuck on stupid, watching the whole thing like it was a bad dream.

...

Later that night, at one in the morning, Reggie sat in his dim kitchen, wearing boxer shorts and a tight, food stained wifebeater. His fat Polish wife was knocked out upstairs, snoring like a freight train. Reggie sat hunched over the table, cradling his fourth glass of Maker's Mark, a tall can of Samuel Adams sweating next to him.

The booze took the edge off the embarrassment he'd felt earlier. Sure, Cyr clowned him in front of everybody, but most of the squad was riding with him. They thought just like he did. Bigots or not, they were his tribe. That shit made it a little easier to swallow.

11

Omaha, Nebraska, was frozen in seventeen-degree weather, and the cold rain hit like razor blades. Out on the farm, goats, pigs, and cows picked through the mud behind a rusty fence. Chickens scattered across the yard, pecking at bugs, while horses snorted, and roosters screamed into the morning. Winds whistled through the crops, shaking the trees, and the old skeletons of barns and buildings groaned with every gust. Buddy hated the place, but the law had him on the run. Nebraska was a long way from home, but this rural ghost town kept him out of sight, and for now, that's all that mattered. It was just Buddy and his twelve-year-old surrogate son, Marcel, out here—living low, running from demons.

"In this life, you gotta choose your battles," Buddy said, yanking Marcel out the mud. "But if a war comes lookin' for you, you aim to kill. No second chances."

Buddy had just slammed the boy into the dirt, planting him hard enough to rattle his ribs. Marcel's hands and feet were numb, mud sticking between his toes since barefoot was how Buddy trained him—no exceptions. Whether running, fighting, *or jumping, Marcel had to learn to move without shoes. Buddy didn't believe in mercy.*

"I... I hear you," Marcel stammered, his breath ragged. His little body shook like a leaf. Teeth chattering, skin scarred, frozen in the kind of cold that reached into your bones. Buddy, though, didn't seem fazed. Not by the cold. Not by nothing.

Keenan Jackson, better known on the streets as Charles 'Buddy' Turner, was a beast bred by war. His old man had taught him Lethwei, Krav Maga, and many other ways of survival, bringing home tricks from World War II reconnaissance missions. And now, Buddy was passing that same discipline down to Marcel, who'd been in his care since he was just an infant.

Buddy wasn't no saint. He'd run with a crew back in the day —his childhood homeboy, Darnell Beck, and Darnell's woman, Lynette Watkins. They got money any way they could—banks, card games, dice, corner stores. If it had value, Buddy, Darnell, and Lynette took it. Their streak ran for six years, leaving nothing but wreckage in their wake. But that last job in L.A.? That one went south.

It was supposed to be clean—in and out, no bodies. But it ended with security guards and civilians laid out in pools of blood. Cops were everywhere. Darnell and Lynette put up a fight, dropping four officers, but backup came in blazing and sent fifty-five slugs into them.

Buddy saw the writing on the wall and peeled off before it all went bad. "Ain't no glory in dying for nothing," he'd always say. The next thing he did was scoop up the couple's newborn son— Marcel—from a friend's crib. And from that moment, it was just him and the kid, running.

"Power equals weight times speed," Buddy growled, pacing in front of Marcel. "Throw a jab if you gotta, but when you go *for the knockout, you swing for a motherfucker's head. That's your home run."*

Buddy squatted next to him, wiping some mud off the kid's face.

"You feel me? If you get a clean shot, aim for the head. Make it count."

At twelve years old, Marcel barely weighed 120 pounds, soaked in rain and tears. He was tough, but Buddy made sure "tough" wasn't enough. The scars on Marcel's arms were still raw from the cold wind cutting through his skin. If the boy ever asked Buddy to stop, all it did was make the man double down.

Buddy knew Pattie, his girlfriend, hated how he treated Marcel. She wanted to baby the kid because she couldn't have no kids herself. But Pattie never said a word. She knew Buddy had his reasons. And even now, Buddy could feel her standing in the doorway, watching him work Marcel into the ground. Her stare burned into his back, and he figured it was time to let the boy breathe.

"Alright, little man," Buddy said, standing over Marcel. "Say the creed, and we'll call it for today. Get inside, get some food."

Marcel's stomach growled so loud it hurt. He couldn't feel his fingers, couldn't feel his toes. The cold gnawed at him, but his mind was sharp. Sharp enough to know if he got it wrong, they'd stay out here until he dropped.

"No matter the fight, battle, or war," Marcel whispered through frozen lips, "implement a counterbalance strategy. Never lose my presence of mind."

Buddy grinned. "That's it. You got it, kid."

...

The hospital room was cold, but that wasn't what had

Marcel shaking. He clung to Buddy's lifeless body, sobbing into his chest, tears pouring down like a busted faucet. Buddy was gone. His big, hard hands that once pushed Marcel through hell now rested still and cold.

Nate stood nearby, fresh tears rolling down his own face. It had been nearly an hour since Buddy took his last breath, and Marcel hadn't left his side. Buddy had made Marcel promise he'd be there, and Marcel had kept that promise.

...

When Nate stepped out of the apartment to give Marcel some space, the boy's grief took over. When Nate came back a few hours later, Marcel was curled up on the floor, passed out, with an empty bottle of Hennessy still in his grip.

Nate didn't say a word. He grabbed a blanket, draped it over Marcel, and let his friend sleep off the pain.

Because Nate knew. He knew exactly what that kind of hurt felt like.

12

The scorching hot, Nevada sun promised no rain anytime soon. The outside of the crib on Cedar Street was an eyesore. It looked like it should've been condemned years ago. The inside was a different story-lavish and high-end. An 85-inch Samsung TV hung over a fake fireplace, the glow giving the room a weird kind of warmth. Paintings-some Picasso, a couple Van Goghs, covered the walls painted in wild, mismatched colors. A black leather sectional wrapped the room, piled with pillows in every shade under the sun. The side tables displayed statues. Julius Caesar's cold marble stare on one, and the somber face of Atticus on the other.

Two blonde, blue-eyed girls, barely out of high school, were laid out on the sectional, all giggles and high. They were gone, strung out on meth, and too lost in the high to see the danger creeping around them. They didn't even flinch when, at one point, they locked lips, sharing a hungry, passionate kiss. Lulu was right there, not even phased. The girls believed every lie Lulu fed them, thinking she was just some rich lady who wanted company. After

Lulu took them out shopping, filled their bags with clothes, and kept their drug cravings fed, the girls saw no reason to leave.

Lulu Nichols, petite, redbone, pushing late thirties, sat on the far end of the sectional like a queen on her throne. Her cornrows were laid tight, scalp shining between the braids. Dark brown eyes sat heavy under bags from nights spent scheming. She moved like a shy chick, quiet and clueless about the world. But that was cap-her heart was cold, filled with venom and hate. She'd do anything to secure the bag, even if it meant grinding others into dust.

Lulu was top-tier in the sex-trafficking hustle, a recruiter with a rep. She leaned back, cool as a fan, without a worry in the world. A working girl, one of her best earners, had just handed her a stack, but it was light. Short for the second time this month. Lulu wasn't the type to let that slide. She could've made a scene, but not tonight. Not in front of fresh meat. She put on a mask of patience and ran some game instead.

"Look, Abby. It's cool," Lulu said, voice smooth like honey. "You brought me something, and that counts. But this is just between us, ok? Go back out there, give it two more hours, and make up what's missing. We're good after that."

Abby nodded quick. Her light brown eyes, red from crying, locked onto Lulu with desperate hope. She had freckles dusted across her nose, and an ugly scar sliced across her once pretty face. The scar wrecked her confidence, made her feel like damaged goods. Abby wiped her face with the back of her hand, smearing tears and snot. Relief poured over her as she pressed her hands together like she was praying.

"Thank you," she whispered, tears streaming again, a

fresh glob of snot slipping toward her lip. Lulu smirked inside, almost amused Abby hadn't pissed herself yet.

"Go make me proud, Abby," Lulu said, voice still slick and steady. "You got potential. Develop it, and you could sit where I'm sitting. Sure, that scar's a bitch. But your charm? That's your weapon. If you can get my pussy wet with just words, then a man out there won't give a damn about that scar. But listen, people in my shoes?" Lulu leaned in just slightly. "They don't let this kinda thing slide twice. They'll come for you. Or worse, your people. Don't forget that."

Abby nodded fast, swallowing hard. She heard the message loud and clear. The threat wasn't loud; it oozed out of Lulu's mouth, quiet and deadly. But Abby was stuck. She had nowhere to go. No family. No cash. No backup. Lulu provided everything.

The second Abby shuffled out the door, Lulu stood up and called toward the back.

"Billy! Get in here."

It didn't take long for Billy to show. Tall, built like a linebacker, he moved with quiet menace. The teens on the couch perked up, eyes wide and locked on him. Billy had that kind of effect. His skin was smooth and dark, his jaw rough with a five o'clock shadow that added to his dangerous charm. He wore black windbreaker pants that clung to him in all the right places, leaving little to the imagination. The girls stared, biting their lips.

Billy was more than just eye candy. He was Lulu's first cousin and a problem. A registered sex offender, a convicted rapist, a career scumbag. His job was to break these girls in. Lulu gave him a nod, a silent order. Get these girls out of her sight for a bit. Billy didn't need any more encouragement.

Once the room was empty, Lulu pulled out her phone, dialing a number from memory.

"Finish her off," Lulu said the second the call connected. Her voice was ice-cold now, no trace of the smooth charm she'd used on Abby earlier.

"She ain't bringin' in no money with that fucked up face. Give her a big blast to send her off.

She hung up, not waiting for a response. Lulu stood there for a moment, the hum of the TV filling the silence. Business was business. There were no second chances.

13

The rain finally cut the heatwave's chokehold. Days had passed without a drop, and if this was California, wildfires would've already taken the place over. But for Marcel, the downpour was a gift-a perfect cover. He knew the stash house goons weren't feeling it. No one wanted to stand watch in a storm like this. That just made it easier for Marcel to make them even more miserable. Marcel and Nate sat in Buddy's black van, eyes locked on the safe house across Dikeman Street. Binoculars in hand, Marcel tracked the three flunkies posted up. He'd been watching them for weeks. Nate was tagging along by choice, insisting on being part of this run. Marcel didn't argue. Kid wanted in, fine. He'd see how real things got soon enough.

Marcel knew the crew by heart now: one was tall and skinny, another short and fat, and the third-a thick, dark-skinned dude-was clearly the ringleader. The fat one was always on some clown shit, but the muscular one was the real problem. Right on schedule, a black Acura crept up. A fat, biracial chick hopped out, huffing from the effort of hauling her weight up the porch steps, and plopped down on the third one like she owned it. The lanky dude slid into the passenger seat of the Acura, and the fat dude jumped in the back. Yesterday, the same driver rolled through in a Toyota Sienna. The routine was the same, just another night, another swap.

Nate sat tense, beads of sweat rolling down his face despite the rain cooling the air. His leg bounced, and his teeth rattled. Marcel noticed but didn't say a word. The kid had been keeping his head above water since his mom passed, helping at the apartment, even putting food on the table with his EBT card. But tonight was different. Nate wasn't ready for this. He saw Marcel gear up, sliding on gloves, strapping into a bulletproof vest, and tucking a Glock into his waistband, and the kid almost folded on the spot.

"You good?" Marcel finally asked, knowing the answer.

Nate shifted uncomfortably. "Victor's got a piece, Marcel. Man's dangerous as fuck. You sure this ain't too much?"

Marcel gave him a hard look.

"And he's sittin' on that porch right now with a chick who damn near fainted getting out the car. This is our shot."

Nate swallowed, clearly out of his depth. Marcel handed him a pistol.

"I don't need you to ride inside with me, just cover my back. You asked for this, so earn your keep."

Nate inspected the clip, making sure it was full. His hands trembled, but he nodded.

Marcel leaned closer. "It's insurance. If it goes left, you know what to do. But let me be straight with you: I ain't no parent, and I damn sure ain't your role model. You want to ride with me, you do it knowing that."

Nate stared down at the piece. "I got you, Marcel."

Marcel gave a slight nod, then slipped out of the van and into the rain, moving like a shadow through the storm.

...

On the porch, Linton fidgeted, pissed at the world.

"I could cook better than that taco-eatin' motherfucker, but instead I'm here with your fat ass in the rain."

Sophia rolled her eyes, unfazed.

"You out here 'cause that's all you good for... lookout duty."

Linton grinned, licking his lips as his eyes ran over her heavyset frame. Her attitude didn't bother him; the way her breasts swelled beneath her wet shirt had him thinking twice.

"Fuck all that. Let's hit a room after this."

Sophia sucked her teeth.

"I'd love to, Lint. You know that. But you smashed Myra, and that bitch got herpes. I'm straight."

Linton flinched, his smile fading fast. "You believe everything you hear?"

Sophia wasn't buying it.

"My son's father used to work for the department of public health. Myra has papers on her. She been dirty for a minute."

Linton kept a poker face, but inside, he was panicking. He'd been raw with Myra more than once.

"Shit, I ain't never touched that bitch like that. Niggas lie, you know that. She told me she was on her period, so we didn't even go there."

Before Sophia could respond, she caught sight of someone approaching through the rain. A slim figure, hood up, moving too steady to be lost. Linton noticed her shift and turned around.

"You lost, fam?" Linton asked, hand hovering near his waistband. The man stopped at the porch.

"Nah. Lookin' to cop. Y'all the only ones out here, right?"

Linton narrowed his eyes.

"I don't know you. Get the fuck on before you get hurt."

The man shook his head.

"If y'all pushin' product, what's the issue?"

Sophia stood up, glaring.

"You talkin' real reckless."

Linton pulled his gun and pressed the barrel to the man's forehead.

"You got a death wish, nigga?"

The man smiled.

"Maybe."

Before Linton could react, the man's hand flashed. A silver blade sliced through the air, knocking the gun loose. Marcel's other fist connected with Linton's throat, crushing his windpipe. The goon staggered, choking on his own breath. Marcel swept his leg out, and Linton's skull hit the pavement with a sickening crack. Blood oozed from the gash, pooling fast. Sophia screamed and lunged at Marcel. He dropped back, slamming her head-first into the asphalt. She went limp, unconscious from the head trauma.

Linton wheezed, trying to crawl away, but Marcel was on him. He grabbed Linton by his shirt and drove a final blow into the side of his skull, severing an artery in Linton's brain. Linton's body jerked once, then went still. Marcel dragged the lifeless man into the overgrown grass, disappearing him into the weeds. Without missing a beat, Marcel scooped up Linton's gun, grabbed Sophia by her hair, and hauled her toward the front door. The barrel pressed against her temple kept her in line.

...

Inside, the bass-heavy thump of reggae music filled the air. A pitiful whimper echoed from a corner where a puppy lay curled up in a filthy cage. Bart and Kent were in the living room, surrounded by bags of heroin and fentanyl. Bart, a thick dude with a lazy eye and wild afro, loaded guns while Kent, fresh from the kitchen, peeled off a sweaty mask.

"Man, if that dog don't shut the fuck up, I'm killin' it," Kent growled, kicking the cage. Bart shook his head.

"Six hours in that cage covered in shit? You'd be cryin' too, dumbass."

Kent ignored him. "What's good with the Mexican? Barry gonna put him on?" Bart snorted.

"He offered dude a couple mill. We ain't seein' none of that."

Kent's face twisted with envy.

"We cook the same shit, and we ain't gettin' a dime? Fuck Barry." Bart's lip curled.

"Nigga, you serious? We killed fiends with that last batch. Barry's keepin' us alive. Be grateful." Kent sneered.

"Or we could kill his ass first."

Before Bart could answer, he noticed movement in the

doorway. Kent saw it too, his hand drifting toward his piece.

"Don't." Marcel's voice was cold steel. "Tell him to drop it, or we all die."

Bart sized him up, then nodded.

"Kent, put it down."

Kent cursed but did as he was told.

"Where's Linton?" Bart demanded.

"Dead," Marcel answered flatly. Kent's hands went up.

"Take what you want and bounce."

Marcel didn't flinch. Two quick shots echoed through the house, each bullet finding its mark. Kent and Bart slumped to the floor, blood splattering the walls like abstract art. Sophia screamed, but Marcel silenced her with a glare.

"You wanna join 'em?"

She shook her head, trembling.

"Get out," Marcel snarled, pulling her license from her pocket.

Sophia didn't wait. She bolted through the kitchen and into the night, sirens wailing in the distance. Marcel stuffed cash into his pockets, scooped up the puppy from the cage, and slipped out the back. By the time he hit Orange Street, Nate was waiting, engine idling. Marcel slid into the van, the puppy shivering in his arms.

"Drive easy," he told Nate.

Nate nodded, and as they cruised back to the crib, the puppy curled into Marcel's lap, already trusting its new owner.

14

Barry's spot, The Gem, was alive and wild. Strobe lights cut through the dark like switchblades, flashing from the club's heart as Barry slid through the crowd outside. The line stretched long, full of people waiting to get patted down by two bald, dark-skinned bouncers built like linebackers. But when they caught sight of Barry, they froze mid-pat, stepping aside without a word. Barry breezed past them, cold as steel, treating them like furniture—no nod, no dap, not even a glance. Just another day.

Inside, waitresses with bodies bought on credit paraded through the packed club, their tiny outfits barely holding them together. Asses bounced and smiles glimmered as they poured drinks priced like rent money into the glasses of hustlers, crooks, and nine-to-fivers looking to feel special for a night. Beyoncé's *All Up In Your Mind* rattled the walls, and the whole floor was a mess of bodies grinding and swaying. Barry slid through them, a ghost among the living, ignoring the shout-outs and grins thrown his way. His mood was nasty, locked tight behind a stone face that told everyone tonight wasn't the night to fuck around.

Barry's target was downstairs, beneath the smoke and noise. His private meeting room sat hidden from the madness, where four of his goons sat waiting like a council of wolves.

The hum of hip-hop and reggae bled through the office walls as Barry scanned the room, his eyes locking onto Sophia. She sat hunched between Dwight, Brody, and Conner, all dressed sharp in suits that fit too well for street soldiers. Barry didn't trust Sophia's story, not yet. Too much heat. Three dealers, all dead, and not just any dealers, but Barry's own people. Whoever did it have skill. Had hands.

Conner leaned back, blowing smoke with a smirk.

"Yo, either shorty's lying, or the boys you had baggin' that work was soft as fuck."

Sophia shot Conner a cold, dead-eyed look.

"If you was there, you would've been laid the fuck out next to them, easy. I know what I saw."

Barry kept his eyes locked on Sophia, quiet, reading her like a card game. The bandages wrapped around her head told part of the story. The way her arms were folded tight over her stomach told the rest—she was shaken, no doubt. She tried to play tough, but Barry could see through it. Witnessing two murders up close wasn't for the faint, and Sophia wasn't built for it.

He crouched beside her, close enough to feel her shaky breath. His hand found hers, warm and steady. He rubbed it gently, a smile creeping onto his face, slow and deliberate, like a cat playing with its prey. Sophia softened, the hardness in her eyes cracking under the weight of his kindness. Barry knew exactly how to work people—knew when to press and when to pull back. And right now, she needed soft.

"Tell me everything," Barry said, his voice smooth but low enough to carry weight. "From the jump. Don't leave nothin' out."

Sophia's eyes, red from weed and whatever tears she'd fought earlier, flicked up to meet his. She exhaled, and the story spilled out, piece by piece. She walked him through the bloodbath on Dikeman Street. The fall to the concrete had her dazed, probably concussed, but she remembered enough. Enough to keep her awake at night for the rest of her life. Dwight had heard the story twice already, and it hadn't changed.

Barry stood, extending his hand. Sophia took it and let him pull her to her feet.

"We're putting a hundred racks on his head," Barry said, glancing toward Dwight.

"What you think?"

Dwight gave a slow nod, a grin tugging at his lips.

"Money makes a lot of noise, bruh. Somebody gon' listen."

Barry turned to Brody and Conner.

"Get her home."

Brody nodded, and Conner gave a grunt of approval. The door clicked shut behind them, leaving Barry and Dwight alone in the quiet hum of the room.

"You sure about this?" Dwight asked, folding his arms.

Barry popped the top button on his shirt, giving himself a little air. "Yeah. It's the right move. Money fuckin' talks."

...

The ride was a silent one. Brody, hands draped over the

wheel of a slick black Tahoe, kept his eyes on the road. His lazy right eye gave him a permanent look of disinterest, but there was sharpness behind it if you knew where to look. Conner, thickset and light-skinned with razor bumps crawling up his neck, rode shotgun. Neither had much to say, and Sophia was grateful for that. She sat in the back, just behind Conner, lost in her own thoughts.

Barry believing her was a win she hadn't expected. She still couldn't wrap her head around how wild the whole thing sounded—the mystery man rolling through, slaughtering everyone in the trap house.

The silence in the SUV was like a blanket, letting Sophia plan her next move. She wanted out—out of the game, out of the life. No more late nights dodging stick-up kids, no more fentanyl fiends dropping like flies, no more cops sniffing around. And no more blood. Watching Kent and Bart die right in front of her was enough to scar her for life. Church was calling. A new life. A fresh start.

15

A misty veil hung over the city, drizzle weaving its way through the air in a slow, lazy dance. The scanner cracked to life—somebody had just stuck up a package store, and now the perp was on foot. Every unit was in on it, the chase lighting up the streets. Sharpe handled the cruiser like it was second nature, tearing through red lights and blowing past stop signs without a second thought. Hayden sat in the passenger seat, locked in his own head. The massacre on Dikeman Street two nights ago still had him stuck. Not that he hung out with them, but he knew of Kent and Bart since middle school. Now, they were stretched out cold in the morgue, riddled with bullet holes. There was another body too, found face down in the tall grass on the edge of the property. It felt like a bad dream, one he couldn't wake from.

"Attention all units, suspect spotted in the area. Description: black male, 30 to 40 years old, six-three, 180 pounds, bald, black windbreaker jacket, blue jeans. Suspect is armed and dangerous. Proceed with caution."

Sharpe leaned into the radio. "Copy that. What's the last known location?"

"Suspect was seen near the bottom of North Main Street, moving up the hill on foot. Use extreme caution—backup is en route."

Sharpe nodded. "We're on it. Over."

He swung the cruiser around hard, tires screeching as he took a sharp turn onto East Farm Street.

Hayden felt the jolt in his bones, snapping him out of his thoughts. The streets out here were wild—young dudes and hustlers posted on every corner, eyes cold and hard from living a life that gave no breaks. But whoever Sharpe spotted wasn't in the original description.

The cruiser rolled to a stop at the curb, and Hayden sat tight, already dreading whatever was about to go down. Sharpe jumped out, his eyes locked on a light-skinned young man rocking a long-sleeve black tee—not a windbreaker. Dude was barely five-ten, a far cry from the six-three suspect.

"This ain't the guy," Hayden muttered to himself, but Sharpe was already on a mission.

"Hands against the wall!" Sharpe barked, his voice sharp.

The kid tensed up, wide-eyed but compliant.

"Yo, man, I'm good, I ain't resistin'!" he shouted, pressing his palms to the wall like he was supposed to.

But Sharpe was already hyped.

"I said, hands against the wall!" he snapped, closing the space between them fast.

Hayden slid out of the car, jaw tight, watching the scene unfold. He could feel the tension rolling off Sharpe in waves. This wasn't the right guy, and he knew it.

"Sharpe, that ain't him," Hayden said, trying to keep his voice steady.

"This is the suspect," Sharpe hissed, his hand creeping toward his holster.

The kid looked around, panic flickering across his face. When he turned slightly, his shirt lifted just enough to show a sliver of skin. That's all it took.

Sharpe's instincts kicked in—paranoia, adrenaline, fear—all boiling over in a split second. Before anyone could stop him, his finger was on the trigger. The gunshot cracked through the air, sharp and final.

The kid hit the pavement hard, his body folding awkwardly as the life drained out of him before his head even hit the ground. Blood pooled beneath him, soaking into the cracks of the street like the city was swallowing him whole.

For a moment, Sharpe just stood there, gun still in hand, frozen like a statue. The shot echoed in his head, louder than anything around him. Reality hit him like a brick wall—he'd fucked up.

"Shit! Shit! I thought—" Sharpe's voice cracked. "I thought it was the guy we were looking for! Fuck!"

Somebody in the crowd shouted, "Fucking pigs!"

The blood on the pavement was spreading fast, and Sharpe's pale face burned red, the shame cutting deeper than the chill in the air.

"What the fuck were you thinking?!" Hayden exploded, stepping toward Sharpe, his voice booming over the growing commotion.

A low murmur rose from the people nearby—then it grew louder, a chorus of anger and fear. Mothers pulled their kids close, faces twisted in horror. Somebody started chanting, low and angry, and others joined in, their voices filled with rage.

Hayden hit up dispatch despite Sharpe calling it in moments earlier.

"All units, accidental ten seventy-one and ten-thirty-three at East Farm Street. Officer involved in shooting. Need backup immediately!"

Hayden clenched his fists, fury bubbling beneath his skin. It wasn't even noon, and Sharpe had already killed a kid and lit the fuse on a riot. All thoughts of the Dikeman Street murders vanished. Now, they had a new body to deal with, one that never should've been a problem in the first place.

"You fucking idiot!" Hayden growled, his voice low and venomous. "You murdered that kid, you piece of shit. This one's on you."

Sharpe shot him a sharp look, his jaw tight. "I followed protocol! He looked like the guy!"

His voice was desperate, teetering between anger and regret.

"I swear, I thought it was a windbreaker!"

Hayden shook his head, disgusted. "Save that bullshit for the captain."

The crowd was getting louder, angrier, closing in. Sirens howled in the distance, but it didn't feel like they'd get there in time. Sharpe looked around, panic setting in. The real suspect had vanished into thin air, leaving them with nothing but a dead kid and a block ready to explode.

And standing in the middle of it all was Sharpe—a bigoted, trigger-happy black cop who just made the worst mistake of his life.

16

Katia blew a long, tired sigh. It had been an hour since her last client bounced. Lucky for her, the one tonight was just some washed-up old man from Finland who didn't want nothing but someone to talk to. Easy work. The baby boomer paid double her quota, and the night was still young. But even with the extra bread, Katia's head wasn't right. Life felt like a one-way trip to nowhere. If something didn't change soon, she was done for.

The place was alive with noise-moans from different rooms, low music playing in the lounge, and whispers floating like cigarette smoke as clients and workers huddled over drinks. Katia sat on the plush bed, clutching the cash she made. Somewhere nearby, Billy lurked, probably watching her and a couple others, waiting to shut things down when they finished.

Freedom felt like a joke, always just out of reach. Every time she thought about it, Sloan's threats ran through her mind like bad memories on repeat. If she ran, he'd have her family wiped off the map. It had her locked, chained without cuffs. And then there was Lulu, playing her role like some devil in heels. To Katia, Lulu was worse than any warden -sick with power, a dealer of misery. Katia saw girls overdose, bodies hit the floor, and rapes that went unchecked under Lulu's watch. It wasn't just the streets that were ruthless-the sex trafficking world was a full-blown hell on earth.

...

Moonlight slid through the cracked blinds, streaking across Abby's scarred face like a grim reminder of everything that went wrong. She lay sprawled on a nasty, stained mattress, her bare skin glistening under the faint light. Trevor hovered over her lifeless body, a dark silhouette in the filthy room. Abby sniffed enough fentanyl-laced dope to put an elephant down. Her lips turned cold and blue; her half-open eyes fixed with tiny pupils that didn't see anything anymore. The gurgling noises she made earlier stopped about five minutes ago.

Abby was gone, marinated in her own vomit and feces on the busted leather couch. The room told the rest of her story. A burner phone with a cracked screen lay next to an ashtray overstuffed with butts. A grimy rose-stem pipe sat within reach, surrounded by the sad leftovers of her life, a life chewed up and spit out like trash.

17

Under the low flicker of the chandeliers, the tables gleamed, draped in crisp white linens. The smell of steak, chicken, and garlic floated heavy in the air, wrapping around them. Marcel kept it real, sharing bits and pieces of his life, leaving out the vigilante shit. When he told Nyomi he used to hustle, moving drugs and guns, and now lived off his savings, doing odd jobs and shifts at a local bodega, her eyes widened just a bit. That look, part surprise, part reassessment, flickered across her face. Her lips parted, words on deck, but not quite ready to launch. Marcel caught it and grinned.

"Relax. We just two people having dinner. I know how folks love to judge status-it's cool. I got no expectations," Marcel said smoothly.

Nyomi talked about her career, the degrees she stacked up, her kid, and the plan to head west. As she spoke, Marcel felt that familiar pinch of inferiority creep in, but his life wasn't built for comparisons. It was a different grind. Still, somewhere inside, he let a sliver of hope take root. He was too real to believe in fairy tales, though her whole vibe was out of his reach. Casual, but classy as hell. She rocked well-fitted jeans that hugged all the right places, a soft, flowing tan blouse that draped just right. Her weave fell halfway down her back, sleek, and edges laid tight. A pair of tan wedges gave her a little height, but she didn't need it. She carried herself with grace that came from knowing her worth.

"Honestly, Marcel, at this point, none of it matters. You could come from royalty, and I still wouldn't have time for anyone. I'm moving soon," Nyomi admitted. Then, with a teasing smile, she added, "But if I didn't know better, I'd think you were some CEO or activist ... or maybe even a dog whisperer."

Marcel chuckled low.

"You funny. But nah, just a man figuring things out."

Nyomi leaned forward; eyes bright with curiosity.

"For real, though. You seem so aware, like life gave you a crash course most people don't pass. Ever think about going back to school? Feels like something you'd be built for."

Her question hung in the air between them, weighty but simple. Marcel's mind danced through dark memories, and for a second, he almost let the truth slip. But there were things too heavy to drag into this moment, and besides, she was leaving. What was the point?

"Nyomi, I got real about life too early," he finally said, "but if you moving, my circumstances don't really matter now, do they?"

Nyomi gave a slow nod. "Fair enough. I respect that."

Before the conversation got deeper, the waiter, a middle-aged Irish man with a friendly smile, showed up with their plates. Marcel shot him a thankful grin as he placed the food in front of them, said a few polite words, and then shuffled off to serve more high-end dishes. After they finished eating, Marcel held the door open for Kayla as they stepped outside. The street was alive with sounds-voices, car engines, the hum of a city never sleeping. Three young goons, no older than twenty, stood nearby, talking loud, half-harassing anyone who walked past. One of them locked eyes with Nyomi.

"Yo, my man," the ringleader called out, eyes glued to Nyomi's curves, "you got yourself a fine one, bruh. Thick in all the right places. Mind if I get a taste?"

Marcel's face hardened, confusion turning into something dangerous.

"Marcel, no." Nyomi touched his arm lightly. "They ain't worth it. Let's go."

Marcel shook his head, dismissing the fools with a wave. They turned away, but as they walked toward the car, Marcel sensed the trouble wasn't done. He didn't have a piece on him tonight, but if the goons tried him, mercy wasn't on the menu.

"It was good dining with you," Marcel said calmly, eyes scanning the street. "Before you bounce to the west coast, we should come back here. I gotta try the bass next time."

Nyomi glanced behind them and stiffened. The three thugs were following, the leader pulling out a blade, his crew flanking him.

"Marcel ... " she whispered. "I see 'em."

Marcel stopped and turned; his shirt unbuttoned, ready for whatever was coming.

"Get in the car, Nyomi."

"You can't be serious, Marcel! It's three of them!"

"Nyomi, get in the car!" Marcel snapped, sharper than he intended.

Nyomi didn't argue this time. She got in, locked the

door, and sat frozen, watching through the windshield. The ringleader sneered, swaggering closer with the knife flashing under the streetlight.

"Y'all ain't leaving till we get what we want. We run a train on that pretty little thing, and maybe we just take your shit instead of your life."

Marcel's eyes narrowed. No more talking.

The first thug lunged, knife aimed at Marcel's gut, but Marcel sidestepped and slammed the kid into a brick wall with a bone-rattling thud. The second one came wild, throwing a sloppy overhand right. Marcel ducked smoothly and came up fast with an uppercut that cracked the dude's jaw, sending him sprawling onto the pavement. The last one, the ringleader, was bigger, built like he spent his days in the gym. He charged, knife in hand, but Marcel was quicker. He leapt, twisting mid-air, and landed a precise blow to the thug's temple, dropping him where he stood.

Inside the car, Nyomi sat stunned, heart pounding in her chest as she watched it all unfold. Every move Marcel made was fluid, deliberate, like violence was second nature. Each punch, each dodge, each calculated strike was a brutal dance of survival, and she could hardly breathe as the last thug hit the ground. A storm of emotions whirled through her-fear, admiration, and disbelief.

Across the street, Conner sat in a parked car, phone in hand, watching the whole thing go down through his windshield. His shock faded as he hit record, capturing every second of Marcel's beatdown.

When it was over, Conner sent the video to Barry before calling him. Barry answered on the first ring.

"Peep that video now. I think we found our guy. This nigga just folded three motherfuckers. That bitch Sophia was telling the truth!"

18

Captain Lark busted through the door like a man on a warpath, his dark skin gleaming under the harsh office lights. Papers scattered off the desk as the door slammed behind him, rattling the frame. Officers Sharpe and Oates stood stiff, looking like two kids caught stealing, pale and frozen in place. Lark's face was cut deep with rage, his voice raw like gravel grinding in his throat.

"Y'all done lost y'all fuckin' minds!" he thundered, the walls catching his voice and throwing it back like a slap. "Somebody's dead! Dead! And that's who you decide to pin it on?"

His fists clenched tight, veins crawling up his forearms like live wires, muscles pulsing beneath his rolled sleeves. His usual cool was gone—his eyes burning like they could set both men on fire.

"You had one fucking job: protect and serve!" Lark sat down hard in his chair, the legs scraping against the floor like a knife dragged across metal. He leaned in, jaw locked so tight his teeth ground audibly, glaring at them like they owed him rent money.

The air thickened with tension, every breath dragging like it carried a weight. This wasn't just a reprimand—this was a reckoning. No more bullshit excuses left. Lark yanked open the drawer, snatched out two forms, and slapped them on the desk with a sharp thwack.

"Badges. Now."

Sharpe's hand trembled as he unclipped the heavy metal badge. In that moment, it felt like a headstone pressed into his palm, something that marked not just his failure but his entire life. He knew it. This wasn't just a fuck-up. This was the kind of mistake that buries careers, the kind that sticks with you like bloodstains on white linen.

Oates, on the other hand, stood rooted like a statue, lips pressed into a thin, bloodless line. His face had drained of all color, but fury still simmered in his eyes, sharp and dangerous. He wasn't saying a word, though. Sharpe had pulled the trigger, and now both had to eat the consequences.

Lark's gaze stayed fixed on them like a hunter sizing up prey, waiting to see if they'd fold—or snap. But the fight had drained out of them. All that remained was the oppressive weight of a mistake too big to run from.

"You're both on administrative leave," Lark growled, voice thick with finality. "Effective immediately."

The room became suffocating, as if the walls had closed in another inch. Oates's shoulders tensed as though he'd argue, but one hard look from Lark shut him down cold.

"You think this ends here? Internal Affairs is already breathing down our necks, and there's a criminal investigation right behind it. If you're lucky, maybe—maybe—you'll see the streets again." Lark's eyes narrowed into a cold glare. "But between me and you, don't count on it."

The silence afterward crushed the room like a vise. Lark leaned back in his chair, the leather creaking beneath him, and stared at them with the exhaustion of a man who'd seen this story too many times before.

"Get out."

Sharpe swallowed the lump in his throat, his fingers lingering on the badge for just a second longer before placing it down on the desk. Oates followed, slow and deliberate, the fury in his eyes darkening with every second. They turned and left, the door clicking shut behind them, leaving nothing but the smell of stale coffee and bitter disappointment in the air.

And just like that, it was over—for now. But the long road of investigations, interrogations, and restless nights had only just begun. Whether they'd ever wear those badges again, or whether they'd end up wearing prison jumpsuits, remained to be seen.

19

Bass-heavy music thumped through the suite, making the crystal chandeliers jitter like they were ready to drop. The place was alive with reckless energy. A pack of teenagers was wilding out in the corner, red cups sloshing as they laughed and talked loud over the beat. Dim colored lights danced across their faces, giving everything an electric, otherworldly vibe. The room smelled like cheap liquor, expensive cologne, and perfume-like a party that had already gone too far but kept rolling. Random bursts of laughter sliced through the noise, turning the whole scene into a messy, chaotic symphony of young, careless living.

Gerard had Journey floating like she was on air. He made her feel like she was the baddest chick in the room, and everyone noticed. At just seventeen, Journey had grown used to turning heads, but with Gerard by her side, every eye in the place was locked on her. The hotel suite's colored lights washed over her smooth, ebony skin, making her glow. She rocked a yellow sundress with big floral prints, moving like a dream, her mother's Louis

Vuitton purse slung over her shoulder, completing the look.

A couple of drinks in, and Journey was mesmerized, hanging on Gerard's every word like he was the star in some hood fairytale. His voice was smooth, confident, like he'd seen everything the world had to offer and still had tricks up his sleeve. Those dark eyes of his deep, calculating pools stayed locked on her, pulling her deeper under his spell.

He leaned in close, fingers brushing hers with intention. Then, without warning, he kissed the back of her hand slow and deliberate, sending a chill up her spine. Journey's smile widened, her heart pounding. Gerard knew the game and played it flawlessly, wearing a crisp button-down blue-and-white shirt with brown khakis, a bottle of Sam Adams in hand, laid-back but sharp.

"I'ma give you the world, baby," he whispered, his tone sweet but commanding. "My love's deep-real deep, and whether you like it or not, you stuck with me."

Journey looked at him, soaking in every feature-the sharp jawline, his rich brown skin setting off the clean white shirt, and that stubble on his chin, just enough to keep him looking a little dangerous. She shifted, heat rising from her chest.

"You gon' give me the world, bae? I don't need all that. I just want you. I don't ever want to share you, and you ain't never gotta worry about any other man."

Her voice was soft, but her words hit with the weight of promise. Gerard pulled her closer, his lips brushing against her ear, the scent of his Dior cologne wrapping her in a haze that made her melt.

"You got me, queen. Ain't nobody else."

Their lips met in a long, hungry kiss, heat radiating

between them. Journey clung to him like she never wanted to let go. When they finally broke apart, Gerard flashed a smile, his teeth neat and perfect, like they were carved just for him.

"I love you so much, baby," Journey whispered, her voice shaky with emotion. "Please don't ever hurt me."

Gerard's expression didn't change, his voice steady and smooth. "Never."

...

The room Journey woke up in was a living nightmare—grimy, cold, and thick with the stench of sweat and shit. Bodies lay scattered across the filthy floor, beaten down by hunger and fear. Shadows clung to the walls, and the soft, pitiful sound of whimpering filled the air like a low hum. Some of the women curled into themselves, their faces hollow, eyes empty. Others moaned quietly, like the broken souls of ancestors dragged across oceans into chains. Journey stirred, her body aching, and a chill gripped her like icy hands squeezing her bones. Her head throbbed as reality set in; a brutal, unforgiving slap to the face. Gerard was nowhere to be found. She twisted her neck, scanning the room frantically, heart hammering in her chest, her breathing quick and shallow. Her mouth hung open in disbelief, her eyes wide, desperate.

Then, a blood-curdling scream shattered the silence.

"Aaaaah! Aaaaah!"

The shrieks were high and sharp, raw with terror. A tall, wiry white man stormed in through the heavy metal door, fumbling with the locks like he'd done it a thousand times. His thick bifocals glinted under the dingy overhead light as he made a beeline for the screaming girl. Without hesitation, he snatched her by the throat, slamming a hard right hook into her gut. The girl folded like a chair, vomiting and coughing blood in the same breath. Right behind him strolled in a tall brunette with piercing green eyes and dark hair pulled back tight. She moved with a mean swagger, like she was born to break spirits.

"Anybody else feel like screamin'?" the woman hissed, her voice cutting through the air like a blade. She yanked out a pistol, cocked it with a deliberate click, and pressed the cold barrel against the girl's forehead. The room fell into a suffocating silence. Nobody moved. Nobody dared breathe wrong. Satisfied with the fear she'd planted, the woman smirked, then stepped back. The two of them, a man and woman, had turned and left, the heavy door slamming behind them with a metallic clank.

20

Nyomi sat at the kitchen table, gripping a glass of Pinot Grigio like it was the only thing keeping her together. The walls felt tighter now, suffocating her in memories that used to bring joy. Every photo on the wall whispered a reminder of what was missing—of Journey, and the black hole her absence tore through Nyomi's heart.

She paced the house again and again, her feet dragging across the old hardwood. Every time she stopped at Journey's room, the sight of the unmade bed hit her like a punch to the chest. That bed was a loud reminder: Journey was gone, and no one knew where. Nyomi had called every friend, scrolled through every post on social media, even called the police. All they gave her was a bunch of weak sympathy, no answers—nothing real, nothing helpful.

As the night wore on, the fear sitting in Nyomi's gut swelled like a tumor. The uncertainty was eating her alive. She wanted to scream, but no sound could do justice to the chaos in her chest. Instead, she stared at her phone for hours, praying it would light up with something. But it didn't. Nothing but the silence of night closing in on her.

Then came the knock. It was sharp and sudden, making her heart leap into her throat. Nyomi shot up from the table, her hands trembling—hope and dread twisted together so tight she couldn't tell one from the other.

She threw the door open, breath hitching when she saw Cybil standing there in her nurse scrubs. That caduceus patch on the uniform looked official, like it might bring answers, but Cybil's face said otherwise. The way she shook her head, slow and heavy, knocked the wind out of Nyomi. Whatever tiny sliver of hope she'd been holding on to snapped like a brittle twig.

"Tell me you got something. Anything," Nyomi begged, her voice raw, her eyes wild.

Cybil stepped inside; her expression weighed down with the kind of sorrow that words couldn't carry.

"Hayden ain't heard nothin' yet from Waterbury or Wolcott police," Cybil said, voice low. "He said they on it, but... ain't nothin' solid come back yet."

Nyomi clenched her fists so tight her nails dug into her palms.

"How the hell does someone just disappear, Cybil? Just... gone, like that? If she was white, she would have already been on the news."

Cybil sat down next to her cousin on the couch, reaching for Nyomi's hand. Her fingers shook as they found Nyomi's. She wanted to say something that mattered, but nothing felt right. Nothing felt enough. All the comforting words that floated through her head sounded cheap. She swallowed her own tears, knowing Nyomi needed strength, not sorrow.

"The cops are doing what they can," Cybil said quietly,

rubbing Nyomi's hand. "But we can't just leave it to them. We gotta move too. Journey's out there somewhere, and we ain't stoppin' till we bring her home. We ain't lettin' go of hope. Not ever."

Nyomi's face twisted, her shoulders shaking under the weight of all the fear she'd been trying to hold back.

"It's been days, Cybil. Days. Every minute out there, she's... she's scared. Or worse." Her voice cracked wide open, and the words came out like they were scraped from her soul.

Cybil nodded slowly, her face hard but kind.

"I know, Nyomi. I know."

Nyomi turned her head away, tears slipping down her cheeks, hot and relentless.

"I just... I need her back. I can't do this. I can't live without her."

Her voice trailed off into a choked sob, and Cybil scooted closer, pulling Nyomi into her arms. She held her tight, the kind of hug that said everything words couldn't. Nyomi's lips trembled against her cousin's shoulder, but in Cybil's grip, they stopped. For the first time in hours, she let herself rest against someone who understood the pain without needing it explained.

And in that silence, with nothing solved and no answers yet, they just held on. Because sometimes, that's all you can do.

21

Barry stood like a brick wall in the basement of one of his downtown Waterbury spots, another club he had under his thumb. His cold eyes swept across the room, locking on each of the grim faces gathered around him. Silence sat heavy in the air, thick like cigar smoke, as Barry leaned forward, letting his presence fill every corner of the room.

"Listen up," he rumbled, his voice low and gritty. The men shifted, drawn in, anticipation mixed with fear flickering in their eyes.

"This motherfucker a straight killer. He took out all three of them niggas barehanded."

Barry let that sink in, scanning their reactions. Faces tightened; jaws clenched.

"Now imagine that motherfucker comin' at us strapped."

Barry paused just long enough to keep the tension tight, then gave a slow, deliberate nod toward Dwight.

"I got three hundred grand. Dead that nigga and its yours."

Dwight stepped forward and dropped the oversized duffle bag onto the floor. When he unzipped it, the cash spilled out like a promise. Barry caught the flash of hunger in their eyes and smirked. Greed was a language these men spoke fluently. He needed them sharp, hungry, ready to earn. They all saw the viral video. They knew the kind of beast they were being sent after. Not one of them was dumb enough to try it up close. They had better sense than that. They planned to handle this problem from a distance, trigger fingers steady.

Barry's voice was calm, controlled.

"Keep it quiet. No dumb shit. No witnesses."

A subtle flick of his hand gave the signal. Without a word, the men turned and moved toward the streets, the weight of Barry's expectations on their backs. Determination was etched in their faces-some for the money, others for the fear of what might happen if they failed. The night outside waited, cold and full of dark intentions. Waterbury's underworld didn't need noise; this was going to be silent and swift, the kind of work that ended before anybody knew it started. Barry sat back, knowing the hunt had officially begun.

22

While Marcel was out there catching wreck in the city, Nate sat slumped over his old, beat-up Acer laptop back at the apartment. Weeks slid by since his mom passed, and it'd been fifty long days since Floyd disappeared. His eyes were bloodshot—half from crying, half from smoking that loud to keep from thinking too much. Nate had a feeling deep in his gut that his brother was gone. No word, no clues, just that Floyd's last move had him heading out to Nevada. Trying to track him down felt like chasing a ghost in the desert—just another tear lost in the ocean.

In the last few weeks, Marcel schooled Nate heavy. He taught him how to grip a burner and shoot straight, though Nate knew his aim still needed work. The fact Marcel had the plug on guns and grenades felt unreal. On top of that, Marcel had Nate in the kitchen, showing him how to whip up a mean Western omelet and under the hood of a car, fixing engines like a mechanic. Marcel even taught him a rear-naked choke—one that could send a man straight to the grave if applied the right way. Nate was becoming more than just some kid fresh out of high school. He was a lookout now, a driver, gun cleaner, and even caretaker for Marcel's dogs. No more wasted time. Nate made a promise to himself that he was going to become indispensable, someone nobody could leave behind.

Later that evening, the streets were live. A group of thick-built dudes leaned against the bodega wall, their eyes sweeping the block with that mix of boredom and menace. Every so often, one of them would step off the wall, pressing up on random people, their low, mean laughter slicing the air like a blade. Nate moved through the crew like he belonged, exchanging nods, daps, and quick brotherly hugs, keeping it light.

Jermaine Sykes was in the cut—a brown-skinned dude with a scruffy afro, rocking a black Nike tee, some flip-flops, and bright red basketball shorts. When Jermaine saw Nate, he gave him a head nod and waved him over.

"What's good, Jermaine?" Nate said, slapping hands and pulling his boy in for a hug.

"You, my G," Jermaine replied, studying Nate like he was trying to figure out what was really going on behind his eyes. "Any news?"

Nate looked down, shook his head slow.

"Nah. Nothing."

Jermaine blew out a long breath, frustration heavy in the air.

"Nate, if you need something, you know I got you, bruh. We gotta keep praying and thinking positive. I know it's easy for me to say, but I ain't letting go of hope, dawg. Floyd's out there somewhere."

Nate nodded, but there was a crease of doubt on his face.

"What makes you so sure?"

Jermaine gave him a look. "Bro, you woke? It ain't just kids and chicks getting snatched for that human trafficking shit. Dudes get caught up too. Floyd told me his new job was in Vegas. That shit screamed red flag. He was hustling hard to stay outta jail, so when that gig popped up, he jumped on it."

The thought of his brother caught up in some human trafficking shit twisted Nate's stomach, but the more he thought about it, the more it felt possible. The streets don't discriminate.

"How the fuck traffickers snatch dudes like Floyd, though?" Nate asked, disbelief still thick in his voice. "He's a beast. Lift weights, shoot guns... he'd lay somebody the fuck out."

Jermaine lit up a cigarette, taking a long drag before answering.

"Opportunities, my nigga. That's how. Same way anybody else gets snatched. People vanish every day. Men, women—it don't matter. And trust me, if somebody took him by force, I'd know."

Nate side-eyed Jermaine, his gaze sharp.

"Then who sold my mom that bad batch?"

Jermaine spat on the ground like the name left a bad taste in his mouth.

"Bart and Kent. But them niggas got murked a few weeks back."

Nate's expression didn't flinch, but inside, rage simmered just beneath the surface. He knew Marcel had been all over that. That was a secret Nate would carry to his grave.

"They'll get replaced," Nate said, voice low and steady, like he was talking about the weather.

"Already in motion," Jermaine replied. "Heard they got

a young Mexican cat pushing that fentanyl. Brought up some of his people to cut down on the ODs. Niggas been dropping like flies all summer, but these Mexicans? They got that recipe. Best outta anybody. They 'bout to make bank."

Nate arched an eyebrow. "How much bank?"

"Millions, bro. And that's just a start. If folks stop dying, they'll flip that into something crazy. A few mil ain't nothing compared to what they 'bout to make." Jermaine flicked the ash off his cigarette. "Oh, and there's a hit out on the dude knocking off anybody slangin' that fent."

Nate's face stayed blank, cold as stone.

"How much they put on him?"

"Three hundred K. Ever since that footage went viral."

A flicker of confusion crossed Nate's face.

"What footage?"

Jermaine pulled out his phone, scrolling until he found the link. He handed it to Nate without another word.

Nate's heart pounded in his chest, but his face stayed locked—calm and unreadable, like he practiced it. On the screen, his boy Marcel was moving like a demon, taking out three goons with nothing but his hands and feet. It wasn't just a fight—it was a massacre, and Marcel made it look easy.

...

When Nate finally made it back to the apartment, he leaned against the wall, exhaling hard. His breath came out ragged, like he'd been holding it in all day. The weight of everything—the streets, his brother, Marcel's world—pressed heavy on him. There was no turning back now.

23

The sweltering Nevada sun beat down like hellfire, roasting the pavement and everything on it. Sweat dripped heavy off the workers' faces, their clothes sticking to their skin like plastic wrap in the unforgiving heat. They dragged and hauled equipment in the hundred-degree oven, working under the sharp eye of armed guards. Hammers banged, saws screeched, and heavy machinery roared-noise that made the air feel just as heavy as the heat. These men weren't working by choice. It was like an old-school plantation with modern tools. The guards held binoculars and guns, watching over these people from all walks of life like they were livestock.

Floyd Lane slammed the hammer against the wall, his heart weighed down by regret so deep it made his chest ache. Sweat mixed with unshed tears on his face, but he kept working. Memories of Nate and his mom hovered over him like a dark cloud. He told Nate at that commuter lot he'd call once he got settled, but that call never came. He couldn't figure out how everything went sideways, how he got played so slick. And now the guilt gnawed at him.

He glanced around, eyes scanning for any kind of way out. His gaze landed on Ivan, the burly Russian guard with a wild beard. Ivan's eyelids sagged from the heat, and for a second, Floyd thought he might doze off. But that moment passed fast. Floyd's heart jumped when Ivan's eyes snapped open. Floyd tore his gaze away and slammed the hammer down harder, working like his life depended on it- because it did. Ivan spotted him though, and that was enough to make Floyd's stomach churn. The guard's nostrils flared, and his breath came out sharp, like he'd been holding it too long. The vodka on his breath hit Floyd before the words even left Ivan's mouth.

"You look too much, boy. You watch like nosy bird," Ivan growled through thick, broken English, each word dragging out slow and threatening. "If I see eyes wandering like that again ... " He let the words hang for a second, like the air was holding its breath. Then he leaned in close, his gun damn near touching Floyd's face. "You die by my gun." The words were ice-cold, even under the scorching sun. Then, without another word, Ivan swung the handle of his Sig Sauer and cracked it across Floyd's face. The metal hit like a freight train, sending Floyd sprawling to the ground.

He hit the dirt with a quiet thud, the kind that made the other workers freeze for just a second before going back to their business. No one could afford to care too much. Floyd tasted blood on his tongue, but he didn't make a sound. He knew better. Ivan's heavy breathing still loomed over him, a warning that didn't need repeating. Floyd wiped the blood from his split lip with the back of his hand, eyes low, and picked up his hammer. His cheek throbbed like a heartbeat, but he pushed the pain down and kept hammering. In this place, stopping wasn't an option.

24

The warehouse was Sloan's spot—a ragged, hollow shell that once moved weight for the city's grind but now sat dead, just like everything Sloan touched. The rusted walls groaned with age, and broken windows let in the wind's cold whistle, a reminder that this place was left for dead a long time ago. Sloan made good use of it. Tonight, this was where debts got paid.

At the table, Sloan's crew sat like wolves in the cut—watching, waiting. Eduardo, shaking like a fiend in withdrawal, sparked a cheap cigar. The flame danced in his bloodshot eyes, eyes that had seen too many long nights running dirty with no way out. He was slick but never stupid enough to cross Sloan—until now. And now Sloan wanted Eduardo to see what betrayal tasted like firsthand, up close.

"C'mon, Sloan... please."

Eduardo's voice came out shaky, just above a whisper, barely holding onto hope like it could buy him one more minute.

Sloan stayed still, posted like a statue. His heavy gold

ring clinked against the scarred wood of the table as he tapped his fingers slow, like he was counting down Eduardo's last moments. The room stayed low, hushed voices drowned in the weight of what was about to happen. Eyes shifted back and forth—everybody in the room knew what it was. Nobody moved, though.

Sloan stood, slow and smooth, like he had all night to deal with this rat. His voice slid through the room, calm as a loaded gun on the table.

"You know what it is," he said, eyes cold and sharp. "You broke the code. Ain't no comin' back from that."

Eduardo's face twisted, fear making him look smaller than he already was. His whole body slumped like he was about to fold in on himself. But it didn't matter—nobody leaves once they step wrong with Sloan.

Trevor leaned back, quiet as a shadow, then pulled a sleek silver burner from his coat. No ceremony, no hesitation. Just a tool for a job that needed doing. The metal glinted in the low light, and for a second, the room went still—like everything stopped to watch the end.

The shot cracked loud and clean. Eduardo's head snapped back, and his body hit the floor hard. The stink of smoke and death hung in the air, but nobody flinched. Nobody spoke. It was just business, and Eduardo's time had run out.

Sloan barely gave the body a glance. His eyes, cold as winter, stayed on his crew. He slid the chair back and sat down slow, like nothing had happened. His words came steady, cutting through the silence.

"Loyalty. That's the only thing that matters. Don't ever forget it."

Around the table, heads nodded. The lesson was clear, and the message would stick.

25

The apartment was dead quiet. Hayden sat at the edge of the couch, jaw clenched, replaying the nightmare over and over in his head like a bad movie on loop. His fists balled tight, knuckles white, trembling just a bit. The look on that young brother's face, wide-eyed and scared, flashed before him like a ghost. He could still hear the crowd's shouts ringing in his ears, feel the heat of it all—the chaos, the disbelief—burning a hole through his chest.

Reggie wasn't in the apartment, but in Hayden's mind, he might as well have been. That fat fuck. His own partner had kicked off the madness, sparking a riot that Hayden knew had the potential to spiral out of control fast. And now here he was, both suspended, no paycheck coming in, sitting in limbo while the department figured out who was going to take the fall.

He sat there gripping the morning paper like it had the answers. His eyes locked on the grainy front-page photo—Reggie's ugly mug caught mid-action, slamming some kid against a wall tagged with wild graffiti. And there Hayden was, standing in the background, looking lost as hell.

LOCAL OFFICERS ACCUSED OF KILLING NINETEEN-YEAR-OLD/ LEADS TO RiOT. The bold headline screamed across the top.

Cybil stood in front of him, arms crossed, worry all over her face. She was studying him, waiting on something, but Hayden just sat there.

"Talk to me, baby. What happened out there?"

Her voice was soft, but there was an edge underneath. She was trying to keep calm, trying to hold him together.

Hayden dragged a hand down his face, frustration thick in his breath.

"It was a mess, Cyb. From the jump, I knew we had the wrong dude. The second I saw him, I knew." He shook his head slowly, the weight of it making his neck ache. "Kept telling Reggie, over and over, but that fat fuck wouldn't hear me."

Cybil took a step closer, her eyes narrowing.

"But how the hell did it turn into a riot?"

"He went in hard," Hayden muttered, almost talking to himself. "Too damn hard. Grabbing the kid, shoving him around like he was trying to prove a point. And then his gun went off. Kid died instantly. And people were out there. People saw that shit." He exhaled, voice low and tight. "They started yelling. You know how that goes. A crowd forms real quick when things look dirty. And once they realized it was the wrong guy, it was a wrap."

He paused, the memory hitting like a punch to the gut.

"We jumped back in the cruiser. They were already throwing bottles by then."

Silence hung between them like a fog. Hayden leaned

back into the couch; the tension coiled tight in his shoulders. He felt Cybil's arms slide around him, pulling him close. She didn't say a word—didn't need to. Just held him.

And for a moment, Hayden let himself sink into her warmth, feeling like he wasn't alone in the storm.

26

Under the Santa Monica night sky, the mansion sat heavy on the coastline, a beast draped in luxury and secrets. Hidden behind iron gates, it breathed power, wealth, and dirt. The waves crashed against the shore, but inside the walls, the real noise was made—masked faces laughing too loud, wine glasses clinking, and schemes weaving through every whispered word. Politicians in custom-made suits chopped it up with hustlers and shot callers, their grins tight, eyes always scheming.

Behind a sleek black mask, a greasy politician locked his eyes on a woman across the room. Her gaze cut through the party like a straight razor, a spark of something dangerous hiding behind an elaborate mask. The politician, a walking stomach with arms, slithered his way over to Sloan. He leaned in close, his breath thick with wine and whatever foul thoughts lived inside him.

"That the one with those eyes?" he muttered, the words heavy with intent.

Sloan smiled behind his own mask, already knowing the game was on lock. His trap was set, and it was snapping shut nice and easy. The night wasn't even deep yet, but business was already booming. Having a top-tier politician tangled up like this was gold.

"You've asked about her before. You already know how I operate," Sloan said, swirling *Domaine Leroy* in a glass fit for royalty.

The politician leaned closer, the hunger in his voice more than just curiosity.

"And you know my position, too."

Sloan gave a nod, the smile never leaving his face. "Overstood. One of my people will contact you soon."

The politician strutted off, chest puffed out, heading back into the sea of power players. Handshakes flew like cards at a blackjack table, each one a deal, each grin a silent contract. Sloan watched him go, feeling a wave of satisfaction settle in his gut. This chump wanted one of his girls—a piece from his collection—and Sloan was going to make damn sure she drained every last bit of life out of him.

He took another sip, his mind already calculating the next move. This was how the game was played, and Sloan was always three steps ahead, making sure every pawn knew its place on the board.

27

The van's tired engine purred low as it rolled through the North End streets of Waterbury. The buildings, once the pulse of a booming city, now slouched like forgotten OGs, their brick faces cracking, windows either shattered or boarded up. Overgrown lots, littered with rusted-out cars and the skeletons of old playgrounds, told stories nobody cared to remember. The hood was a graveyard of memories left to rot.

"So, let me get this straight. There's a video out on me, and it's viral?" Marcel asked, his voice even, like he'd known a storm was coming.

"Yeah," Nate confirmed. "And somebody put a hit on you."

Marcel gave a slow, deliberate nod. "That's some real powerful info, Nate. And who told you?"

"Jermaine. My brother's best homie. Solid dude."

Nate pulled out his phone and showed Marcel the video, his finger steady on the screen as the clip played.

Marcel watched quietly, hands clasped together, eyes locked on the video, taking in every frame. It wasn't just the video—it was what it meant. It was the kind of thing that could tip the scales against him, and Marcel knew the game too well to be caught off guard. They pulled into the backyard of the three-family house they were staying in, the van easing to a stop like it knew it was carrying more than just passengers—trouble was riding with them too.

Marcel exhaled through his nose. He knew this was coming; Buddy warned him when he was young, and every step he took since had carried the weight of that warning. There was always a bill to pay. And now it was time.

"Nate, you need to walk away from all this," Marcel said, turning to face him. "You a good kid. I know you signed up for this, but you need to fall back. You lost your mom, your brother's gone, and you still got a shot at a different life."

Nate shook his head, his jaw clenched.

"You and Buddy didn't walk away from me. So why the fuck should I walk away from you?"

"Because it's the smartest move, Nate. You gotta trust me on this," Marcel said, leaning forward, his tone serious.

Nate's eyes didn't waver. "Nah, Marcel. You the only family I got. I ain't got nobody else, and I ain't leavin'. I can't. I won't."

Marcel studied him for a moment, recognizing the stubbornness, the anger, and the loyalty wrapped up in one. Pushing Nate away wasn't an option. The kid was already knee-deep, and Marcel knew he'd raise hell with or without him. Better to keep him close, keep him sharp.

"You trust Jermaine like that?" Marcel asked, shifting gears. "How well you know him?"

Nate didn't miss a beat.

"I know him well enough. That's my brother's closest homie. If I trust anybody, it's him."

Marcel nodded slowly, filing the information away. He moved into the kitchen, fed Houston and Beam, who immediately started wrestling, bumping into furniture like kids too big for their playroom. Nate followed into the living room, his expression tense, like gears in his mind were grinding but not quite locking into place.

"If they put a hit out on you," Nate said, "we need to figure out who's pulling the strings. Jermaine might know more."

Marcel sat down at the kitchen table, pulled out an ounce of Gelato and got to work. His hands moved with precision, breaking the buds down, rolling the *Raw* rolling paper with the kind of calm that came from years in the game.

"That's exactly what we need him for," Marcel said, licking the edge of the paper and sealing it tight. "We test his loyalty. Then we figure out who's behind this hit."

Nate didn't say anything, but the weight of Marcel's words hung heavy in the room. Marcel knew this was just the beginning. Something was stirring, and he needed all his pieces in place before the real game started. Whatever was coming, Marcel was ready to meet it head-on.

28

LAS VEGAS, NEVADA

In the dim, upscale room, Sloan leaned in close, his vibe slick but dangerous. His smile had too many teeth, more threat than charm. He locked eyes with Katia, and there was no mistaking the message in that cold stare.

"Listen up," he said, voice low and steady, the kind of tone that don't leave room for questions. "Friday night, Planet Hollywood. Room 508. You ain't just sellin' a dream, Katia—you secure that bag. That politician at the party the other night? Frank Spivey. He's the key to millions, and you the one holdin' the lock. Open it."

He let that sit for a second, like a blade pressed just enough to break skin but not bleed. Then he kept going, slow and deliberate.

"Every look, every word, hell, every breath, is either a step up or a straight fall off a cliff. Ain't no room for mistakes. You reel him in, make him feel like he the only man in the world. Make him need you. Make him beg. You know how this go."

Sloan tapped the signet ring on his finger, just once, like it was punctuation, making sure she knew this wasn't just a conversation.

"You got the skills. I seen you work. This right here, though? This gotta be flawless. One slip, one fuck-up..."

He didn't need to finish that sentence. She already knew.

He stood up, smoothing the front of his shirt, his slick smile never slipping.

"Get it right, Katia. Money, power, control, it's all on the table. Don't blow it."

With that, he strolled out, the door clicking shut behind him like the slam of a cell.

Katia stood there, her body rigid like her muscles forgot how to move. Sloan's words buzzed in her head like a hive of angry bees. She knew what that man was capable of. He played it cool, but she seen enough to know he'd kill her people without a blink if things went sideways. That wasn't a warning; it was a fact.

Sloan had put her on display for plenty of rich men before, but this Spivey dude was different. Bigger fish than any of the high rollers she'd been paraded in front of. And Sloan needed this to go smooth.

The sparkle that used to light up Katia's brown eyes was long gone, snuffed out somewhere between the first slap and the last threat. Now all she had was a dull flicker, just enough to keep her from falling all the way into the dark. Outside, life carried on—cars honking, people laughing, music spilling out from the Strip. But in the hotel room? Silence. Heavy as a coffin lid.

Katia thought about her options, not that she really had any. The thought crept in again, like it always did when things felt too heavy: Maybe it'd be easier to end it.

She sat down on the edge of the bed, fingers twisting the fabric of her dress, trying to steady her breath. She had to push that thought away, bury it deep. She couldn't afford to check out—not yet. Not with Sloan breathing down her neck and her family on the line.

29
WATERBURY, CONNECTICUT

"Yeah, fam, you could mark yourself a motherfuckin' celebrity. You just cleared them niggas out—arms, legs, and elbows flyin' and all that shit. You got my respect off top," Jermaine said with a grin, taking a deep pull from the Maker's Mark bottle Nate handed him. "And trust, y'all secret safe with me. Word to Floyd."

Marcel gave a tight smile, playing cool while keeping a mental tally on the man he'd only met four hours ago. Now Jermaine was kicked back in Buddy's old recliner, legs stretched out, enjoying the liquor, smoke, and laid-back hospitality. Nate sat slouched on the far end of the couch, half-drunk and faded, lost in his thoughts. His mind kept drifting to his mother and brother, and for a second, anger sparked when Jermaine mentioned Floyd like he was dead. But Nate swallowed it; tonight was strictly business.

"I appreciate that, brother," Marcel said, his tone even. "But I'm takin' it in for the night. I'm tired as fuck."

"You already know," Jermaine replied, eyes low and slick. "And tomorrow? I got that fire for you. My treat."

"Bet," Marcel said, standing up and leaving Nate, Jermaine, and the dogs in the living room.

Forty-five minutes later, Jermaine peeled himself out of Buddy's chair, stretching and cracking his neck.

"Try not to stress, Nate. Remember we chopped it up about hope at the store. Keep your head right. Believe in the Lord, my dude—anything's possible."

Jermaine patted his pockets, then checked the couch cushions, muttering to himself. "Damn, where's my phone?"

"I ain't seen you with no phone," Nate said, rubbing his temple. "It's probably in your whip."

"Yeah, that's where it gotta be," Jermaine muttered, still patting himself down. "But I'm coming through tomorrow with that fire. I'll hit you up."

Nate walked him to the door and watched as Jermaine headed toward the van. Despite the earlier jokes and drinks, something didn't sit right with Marcel. He told Nate that much without saying a word.

In the dark cargo area of the van, Marcel lay perfectly still, every breath controlled, every muscle tense but ready. Sliding into the van had been smooth, but lifting the phone from Jermaine had taken damn near all night.

Jermaine climbed into the driver's seat with a sigh of relief, spotting his phone in the cup holder. The dim glow from the streetlight splashed across his face, painting a portrait of betrayal Marcel recognized too well.

Jermaine snatched up the phone, fingers flying across the screen. When the call connected, his voice dropped to a low murmur, just above a whisper.

"Yeah, I know where he at. He ain't as low-key as you think. If I get that bag tonight, you can have him... tonight... Yeah, tonight... I'm sittin' right in front of his crib now. Yeah..."

Marcel's grip on the Glock tightened. He didn't expect much from Jermaine, but that shit still stung—plain as daylight, the man was selling him out.

"I ain't sayin' nothin' else till I see that cash. Once I do, it's a wrap. Yeah... I got it... Say no more."

Jermaine ended the call, rocking his head to a tune only he could hear, the hum of satisfaction clear as a bell. Twenty-five minutes later, he pulled the van into a dark spot down the street from The Gem. The old van groaned as Marcel slid silently from the back, his presence looming before Jermaine even realized what hit him.

Jermaine's eyes shot wide, the phone slipping from his hand. His lips fumbled for words. "Wait, I can expla—"

The words barely escaped his mouth before Marcel's right hand exploded across his face, shutting down any chance of talking his way out.

30

The poorly lit, abandoned factory assembly line room sat heavy with tension. The only sound breaking through the silence was the shuffle of restless feet on the cracked cement floor. Jermaine, hands bound tight, sat slumped in a cold, rusted metal chair at the center. His eyes jumped from corner to corner, looking for an exit that didn't exist. A shadowed figure leaned against the peeling brick wall, cool and still, watching. Then he stepped into the light. Marcel. Smooth-skinned but hard in the face, his stare cut through Jermaine like a razor.

"Where he at?" Marcel asked, voice calm, but the weight behind it carried danger that promised no mercy. Jermaine shifted, eyes wide, heart hammering against his ribcage.

"I ... I don't know who you talkin' 'bout," he stammered, though his words trembled, giving him away.

Marcel stepped closer, the space between them shrinking.

"Greenwich, Connecticut. I know he's there. What I need from you is where."

Jermaine's heart raced. He knew Barry would be easy to throw under the bus, but Sloan? Sloan was on another level. Getting caught between those two felt like picking a poison, but in this case, one was more potent than the other. Running out of plays, Jermaine decided it was better to give up Barry than cross Sloan.

"Barry stay out in Belle Haven," Jermaine muttered, voice cracking. "But that's a tight zone, bruh. A nigga like me need a express permission."

Marcel's Glock stayed steady in his hand, the tension building like a coiled snake. Jermaine's eyes drifted left, just for a second, but it was all Marcel needed to see the lie slithering out. A bead of sweat ran down Jermaine's temple, slow and deliberate.

"You lyin'."

Marcel's voice came low and sharp, slicing through Jermaine's flimsy excuses.

"You think I got time for this?"

He stepped in close, the barrel of the Glock hovering near Jermaine's jaw.

"Say it again. Clean."

Jermaine blinked hard, his mind spinning like a roulette wheel with no winning number.

"Man, what I'm tied to is too big for you to break through ... "

Marcel swung the Glock, the butt of it smashing into Jermaine's face. The crack echoed through the room. Jermaine's head snapped to the side, blood dripping from the cut spreading across his cheek.

"Ugghhhh!" Jermaine groaned, spitting red. His body sagged, but Marcel pressed the gun harder into his jaw.

"You got one chance, nigga. One. Tell me somethin' worth hearin', or I'm paintin' these walls with your brain."

Jermaine gasped, the pain waking him up fast. He nodded, swallowing down the fear choking him.

"Sloan. He stay out west. You gon' need an army just to get near him. His pockets run deep, man. Too deep."

Marcel's jaw tightened. The Glock stayed glued to Jermaine's temple, unmoving, cold as death.

"Why he so heavy in the game?"

Jermaine's lips trembled as he struggled to find his breath. Sweat slid down his face, tracing his panic.

"He sell people," Jermaine whispered. "And when he done, they disappear."

The words hit Marcel like a slap to the soul. The image of helpless people, bought and sold like cattle, twisted his gut. Memories of the darkness he'd once stepped into clawed at him, memories he fought to bury. But the idea of Sloan trafficking people made his blood boil. The beast inside him stirred, begging to be unleashed. He took a breath, fought the rage down.

"Now, I got one more question," Marcel said, voice steady but sharp as broken glass. "And if I don't like the answer, you ain't walkin' outta here."

Jermaine tensed, eyes wide, body shaking. Marcel let the threat hang heavy between them. Jermaine nodded, the fear leaking from him.

"What happened to Nate's brother?"

Marcel studied the man close, watching his every twitch. The mention of Nate's brother shifted something inside Jermaine. His hands twitched, and his gaze dropped, the weight of what he carried pulling him down.

"It ... it wasn't personal," Jermaine stuttered. "It was a come-up, bruh. Nothin' more. I needed it, man. I had to get off the block."

Marcel clenched his jaw, muscles tightening as he

fought the urge to pull the trigger. His heart pounded, anger threatening to explode, but he held it together-barely. Marcel circled Jermaine slowly, the floor creaking under his sneakers as he walked. The thought of unleashing Nate on this man crossed his mind. Waking the beast in Nate was risky, but maybe it was the right play.

"You lucky Nate think you solid," Marcel said, voice low and dangerous. "So l'mma let him decide whether you see daylight again. But first," he paused, standing behind Jermaine, letting the silence suffocate the man. "You are about to run that list of playas in your phone. I want all the info in this motherfucker. Anything about Sloan, Barry, and whoever the fuck."

Jermaine's breath hitched as the fear wrapped around him. He knew the kind of man Marcel is. The viral clips of his handiwork played on loop in Jermaine's mind, a grim reminder of how things could end. Jermaine also knew that fucking with Sloan would get him killed, but he had no way out. Stuck between two demons, Jermaine chose the one standing in front of him. He coughed, spitting out more blood, and gave up the passcode to his phone.

"It's all in there, man. Every play. Barry's new cook. The traffickers. Killers. It's all there."

Marcel took the phone, slid it into his pocket, and backed away. He gave Jermaine one last cold look before pulling out his own phone.

"Nate, come to the spot we talked about, right now ... Yeah, that spot ... No time like the present ... A'ight ... See you in a few."

Marcel tucked the phone away, eyes still locked on Jermaine. The factory air felt thicker, heavier, like the walls were closing in. Jermaine sat there, bleeding and broken, knowing that every breath he took from here on out was borrowed time. Whether Nate would spare him or not, that wasn't up to Jermaine anymore.

31

The dim light bulbs strung along the ceiling of the underground bunker flickered like they might burn out any second. Dark orange shadows crawled across the cold concrete walls, soaking up the quiet murmurs and restless shuffling of bodies. The place was bare bones-rows of metal cots lined up like soldiers, each with a thin, rough blanket and a pillow flat enough to feel like you were resting on stone. The air hung heavy and stale, thick with a musty funk. Off to the side, they'd rigged up a makeshift bathroom with hanging sheets, trying to give folks a sliver of privacy in a place that didn't have any.

Floyd sat on the edge of the cot, slow and deliberate as he reached for the shirt tossed over the chair from the night before. There was no hurry in his movements—just the kind of slow drag that comes when you've got nothing left to rush for. Across the room, Ivan watched him, never missing a beat. The gun sitting heavy in Ivan's lap wasn't for show—it was there to remind Floyd of the chains he couldn't see but felt all the same. The look in Ivan's eyes said it clear: Floyd was broken, and everybody in that place knew it.

Floyd climbed the steel staircase with Ivan trailing behind him, the clang of each step echoing like a slow march to nowhere. Down in the bunker, day and night blurred together into the same grim haze. But when Floyd hit the surface, the blast of desert heat let him know it was morning. The sun was already beating down like it had a grudge, and Sloan's men were busy herding the enslaved crowd into vans. Their faces were as lifeless as the cracked ground beneath their feet.

A black Hummer rolled up, tires grinding against the sand, sending a cloud of dust spiraling into the dry air. The beast of a vehicle came to a stop, looking as out of place as luxury always does in a wasteland. Inside, Sloan lounged in the backseat, all relaxed like the devil himself dressed in silk. His sharp eyes scanned the desert with a predator's ease, sizing up the scene with the cold calculation of someone who'd done it all before.

Beside him sat a young woman, stiff as a board. Her skin and eyes told the story of a mixed heritage, each feature perfectly placed, but the tension in her body was louder than her beauty. She sat like she knew the eyes of every man around were on her, but she never gave them anything to work with.

The door opened, and Sloan stepped out into the desert heat without missing a beat. The woman followed, silent as a graveyard, and the men circling the van were already moving in sync with Sloan's orders. His voice cut through the dry air, sharp and direct, laying out commands with the smooth precision of a general running his camp. Floyd heard the words, but they barely registered. His focus was locked somewhere else—on her.

Floyd's eyes stayed on the young woman, following every shift in her stance, every glance she gave without meaning to. Something about her gnawed at him, like a memory banging on the door of his mind, demanding to be let in. The harder he stared, the clearer the picture became until the truth hit him like a brick.

Sloan flicked his wrist, gesturing for the woman to get back inside the Hummer. She moved without hesitation, slipping back into the cool, air-conditioned cocoon as Gus, Sloan's driver, waited to pull off. Sloan followed, his hand lazily waving in Gus's direction to signal him to drive.

Floyd stood there, heat pressing down on him from all sides, but he didn't feel it. His heart pounded like it wanted to break out of his chest. That woman wasn't just anybody; he knew her. Not from chance or some passing encounter. She was the girl from the flier, the face Benji had clung to like a lifeline through every long night in that cell.

She was more than a name to Benji—she was the reason he never stopped planning, never stopped sharpening the rage inside him like a weapon. Floyd could still hear Benji's voice in his head, talking about her like she was royalty. After all, she was the queen of hearts from that deck of Connecticut "Cold Case" playing cards they used to shuffle through in prison. Every time Floyd held that queen in a game of Spades, it was like she was staring back at him, daring him to remember every detail. And now she was here, right in front of him, flesh and blood under the desert sun.

Floyd's mind was racing, trying to make sense of it all. But there was no time for thinking—just knowing. And what he knew, without a doubt, was that there was no way in hell he was letting this go.

The Hummer's engine rumbled, tires kicking up sand as it rolled away. Floyd stood frozen for a moment, heart hammering against his ribs. He'd made up his mind, just like that. There was only one way forward; he had to get to her. And he would, no matter what it took.

32

ate stood stone still, his eyes locked on Jermaine, cold and unforgiving. Each slow, heavy breath was a silent warning. The weight of Jermaine's confession sat heavy between them, thickening the air. Without a word, Nate made his move- three long strides- and had Jermaine by the throat. His big, calloused hands squeezed like vices, crushing down on Jermaine's windpipe. Every muscle in Nate's arms flexed tight, fueled by pure rage and years of bottled-up pain. Marcel stood back, watching as Nate's fingers dug deep into Jermaine's neck, pressing hard on his Adam's apple. The choke was relentless. Jermaine's legs jerked beneath him, his breath coming out in sharp, desperate wheezes. But Nate wasn't letting go.

Marcel slipped up, quiet but deliberate, placing a firm hand on Nate's shoulder.

"Enough, Nate." Marcel's voice cut through the moment, calm like a loaded gun. "We need him alive. Think bigger. Your brother could still be out there. He might be the key that blows this whole thing wide open."

Marcel's words hit Nate like ice water. It wasn't just

revenge-it was bigger than that. Slowly, Nate's grip loosened, though his jaw stayed clenched tight. He took a step back, breathing hard, like a man coming out of a trance. Jermaine crumbled to the ground, gasping and wheezing, blood and snot running from his nose. His body convulsed in pain, and before he could stop it, he soiled himself right there on the floor.

Nate glared down at him, disgust flashing in his eyes. And just like that, before Jermaine could even catch a full breath, Nate snapped his foot forward, driving his boot deep into Jermaine's gut. The kick landed hard, folding Jermaine in half as he puked up everything he'd eaten. Marcel watched in silence, his eyes unreadable. Jermaine rolled over, groaning and clutching his stomach, barely able to move. And Nate just stood there, towering over him, chest rising and falling slow and steady, his fury simmering just beneath the surface.

33

Dwight paced back and forth in his elderly mother's apartment, his tall frame casting long shadows across walls worn from time. The hum of the city outside barely touched the stillness inside. He stopped abruptly and turned to Gat, a tall, light-skinned man known for his aim and cold-blooded loyalty. Gat stood quiet, waiting like a loaded gun, ready for Dwight to pull the trigger with a word.

"Who was on the call?" Gat asked, his voice steady, eyes sharp.

Dwight cut his pacing and fixed his gaze on Gat.

"Jermaine," he said, his voice deep, heavy with meaning. "He said he knows exactly where the target is. If he's right, he needs that bag of money. But first, you gotta get confirmation."

Gat gave a slow, measured nod. His face didn't move, but everything about him said he understood.

"And if I don't get that confirmation? If something's off?"

Dwight's lips curled into a slow, grim smile.

"Then you already know what to do. If anything, even the slightest thing looks off—don't hesitate. We can't afford mistakes. Not with this shit."

Gat nodded once, the unspoken agreement between them solidified.

"Got it," Gat said, his voice as firm as a locked bolt. He turned on his heel, the bag of money slung over his shoulder like the promise of a dirty payday.

Dwight watched him head toward the door, then added, "I'm sending Connor to scope out the spot. Just to make sure everything's clean."

Gat didn't respond—he just disappeared into the night.

Alone now, Dwight stood in the silence, thinking of all the ways this could go wrong. The stakes were too high, and they were all playing for keeps. He pulled out his phone, his fingers steady as he dialed.

"Barry," Dwight said, voice low and controlled. "Our problem might be done soon."

...

Barry paced in his private study, the glow of the city creeping through half-drawn blinds. His hand shook as he poured himself another drink, but it wasn't the liquor causing the tremor. Every report of a dead worker, every empty lab, was like dollars burning in his pocket. A goddam vigilante was out there, costing him everything-bit by bit, blow by blow.

He slammed the glass down on the desk, amber liquid splashing over the edge.

"Keep your head down," Barry growled into the phone, his voice a razor's edge between rage and control. "That vigilante's gunning for us. Don't do anything stupid and don't make this worse. Stay low. Stay alive."

On the other end of the line, at least thirty-five miles away, a young Mexican cook stood in a kitchen thick with the smell of danger. He didn't say much—just listened to Barry's silence between the words, knowing exactly what that silence meant.

...

Gat's boots crunched on the gravel path at Long Hill Road Park. The weight of the cash was heavy against his side, but it wasn't just money—it was a promise. He scanned the open field, bathed in the amber wash of dusk, taking in every detail like a hunter tracking prey. His eyes landed on a sleek black BMW parked off to the side, its windows dark and unreadable.

Something about the car pulled Gat closer. He crept up to it, slow and cautious. When he reached the window, he saw Connor slumped over inside, still and lifeless. Head cocked to the side, eyes glazed over with death.

Gat's stomach tightened, but his expression stayed hard. There was no room for shock, only instinct. His hand went to his phone, fingers brushing the cold surface like it could pull him out of the mess he was standing in.

Then it happened—a gunshot, sharp and precise, cutting through the quiet like a blade. Gat didn't even get a chance to react. The bullet found his forehead, ending everything in one brutal second. He dropped, lifeless, crumpling to the ground.

Across the field, Marcel lowered the sniper rifle, his face unreadable in the growing shadows. Beside him, Nate moved with the same cold efficiency. They broke down the rifle in silence, their hands working as one—no wasted motion, no words needed.

They exchanged a glance. Nothing sentimental, just a confirmation that the job was done. With that unspoken understanding between them, they disappeared into the night, leaving nothing behind but the silence of a mission accomplished.

34

The soft glow from a crystal chandelier cast a dim, warm haze over Sloan and Lulu's bedroom. Heavy velvet curtains draped the expensive windows, framing the garden outside. The twilight spilled over the polished oak floors like the last sip of cognac, smooth and dark. The marble vanity and claw-foot tub in the bathroom gleamed, untouched, waiting like a shrine to the good life they lived.

Lulu's dress barely held on; the lace stretched tight over her curves. Her thick, dark nipples pressed against the white fabric, teasing the dim light. She wasn't shy about her body. Sloan lay beside her, stiff like a corpse with his mind elsewhere. He was caught up in a whirlwind of grim thoughts, all centered on a man he hadn't even met. But that didn't matter. Sloan wanted him dead.

He had plans. Dark ones. That man was a serial killer who'd slipped between the cracks, leaving bodies that nobody ever found. But Sloan knew the truth. That man, Richard, was more than a killer. He'd cleaned up after Sloan and Lulu, taking care of things that needed to disappear-bodies, secrets, sins too dirty to leave behind. But tonight, all Sloan could think about was putting Richard in the dirt. Sloan, increasingly paranoid as his empire expanded, saw Richard Hahns as a weak link, aware that the necrophiliac's crimes could expose both him and Lulu's involvement in countless murders and kidnappings. While Richard remained alive, Sloan meticulously plotted ways to eliminate him, knowing it was the only way to fully protect their operation from collapsing under scrutiny.

Lulu shifted beside him, sensing the storm brewing in Sloan's silence. The argument between them had been going on for hours, back and forth like a bad remix on repeat. But she wasn't backing down. She never did.

"He's my brother, Sloan. He is off limits!"

Sloan looked at Lulu with ice in his eyes.

"He ain't your real brother. Y'all don't even share the same gene line, so why the fuck does it matter?"

Lulu sat up in bed. She knew herself to be a heartless bitch, but she met her match.

"What the fuck do you mean why does it matter? He may not be my brother by blood, but he's been there for me. He stopped our foster mom's alcoholic boyfriend from raping me...for good! I will never forget that. You think getting rid of him is gonna fix everything?" she said, her voice low but sharp, cutting through the thick air of the room.

Sloan propped himself up against the headboard. The air was thick with silence. He reached for his cigarettes on the nightstand, the flicker of the lighter briefly illuminating his furrowed brow. A heavy sigh escaped his lips as he inhaled deeply, the smoke swirling around him like a fog.

"It's not about fixing everything," Sloan replied, his

tone cold and deliberate, "it's about survival. Richard's a liability. If he talks, we're fucked. YOUR fucked."

"He's kept his mouth shut this long!" Lulu shot back. "And he's not even a suspect in anything. He's never even been arrested a day in his life! Your paranoia is getting fucking ridiculous!"

Sloan turned his head to look at her, his eyes dark with frustration.

"The stakes are higher. Much higher. The cops are sniffing around too close, and Richard's got more dirt on us than anyone else. If they get to him, it's over. You think he'd go down without dragging us with him? He knows too much, Lulu."

Sloan took a deep drag from his cigarette, the smoke curling around his face as the tension in his shoulders coiled tighter with every puff. The bedroom walls felt like they were closing in, the air thick and suffocating. Frustration clawed at him, and he couldn't sit still any longer. He shoved himself off the bed, his movements jerky and sharp, the weight of his own thoughts bearing down on him like a vice.

His footsteps echoed in the quiet residence each step heavy, deliberate, carrying the fury that churned inside him. Reaching the bathroom, Sloan didn't hesitate. The door slammed shut with enough force to rattle the hinges, the sound cutting through the stillness like a gunshot.

Lulu didn't even flinch when the front door slammed a few seconds later, the vibrations running through the walls but not touching her calm. Her mind moved quickly, calculating, and she reached for her phone with practiced ease. Her fingers found Richard's number, her nails tapping against the screen with a steady rhythm. The line rang, but the response was the same as always, straight to voicemail. Typical Richard.

She leaned back against the headboard, the cool wood pressing into her spine, and lit a cigarette of her own. The first drag settled her nerves, the smoke curling around her like a veil. Thoughts rolled through her head, sharp and dangerous. If Sloan snapped and decided to break the unspoken rule they lived by, the one that kept Richard breathing, then there wouldn't be room for hesitation. Her lips curled into a faint smirk, but there was no humor in it, only resolve. If Sloan went there, if he crossed that line, she knew what she'd have to do. Killing Richard would be a betrayal of their arrangement, but if Sloan made himself a threat, there wouldn't be room for negotiation.

She dragged on the cigarette again, her eyes narrowing as the smoke lingered in the air. Sloan's anger was like a ticking clock, each second bringing him closer to a decision she couldn't afford to ignore. If it came to that, she'd be ready.

<h1 style="text-align:center">35
CONNECTICUT</h1>

The day dragged, heavy and unyielding, as Hayden sat slouched in his living room. The TV was off, and a glass of whiskey sat untouched on the table beside him. The weight of that innocent kid's murder pressed down hard, suffocating him in the silence. Then, his phone's shrill ring cut through the stillness, pulling him out of the whirlpool in his mind.

It was Kurt Cyr, his voice buzzing with a weird mix of excitement and concern.

"Yo, Hayden. I know you've been scrollin' Facebook. There's a video floatin' around—some dude takin' out three guys by himself. I'd bet my badge this is the same guy that's been droppin' these fentanyl dealers. Log in, man. I just inboxed you the link. Call me back."

Hayden felt a switch flip inside him. Even on administration leave, his instincts snapped into place. He clicked the link Kurt had sent. The video was shaky, grainy, like it had been recorded on the fly, but the action was crystal. A brown-skinned man moved through the young men like he'd been born for it, handling them with cold precision, every move trained, every blow fueled by something way deeper than anger.

But it wasn't just the man that caught Hayden's eye. There, caught in the chaos for a split second, was a familiar face. Nyomi. The image hit Hayden like a punch to the gut. She rolls with someone capable of this kind of violence? It didn't sit right. The Nyomi he knew wasn't tangled up in street wars or vigilante justice. But there she was, and not the quiet, moody Nyomi he'd been seeing lately. His wife's cousin had a spark in her, a slight smile that was almost foreign compared to the heavy cloud she'd been under since Journey went missing.

The video was a few weeks old. A lot could've changed since then—Nyomi's vibe definitely had. She'd been moving different, weighed down with each passing day Journey stayed gone. But seeing her in that clip set off alarms Hayden couldn't ignore.

He hit pause, snapshotted her face from the footage, and slid his phone into his pocket. The wind howled outside, throwing rain against the windows, but Hayden didn't care. He grabbed his keys and bolted out the door, the storm raging in step with his thoughts.

...

Cybil had called every hospital in Connecticut, even reached out to the medical examiner in Farmington, desperate for any news. All week long, volunteers and police had searched for Journey. Nothing. No leads, no sign of her. Today, frustration had driven her and Nyomi to even darker thoughts. When the medical examiner's office called back to say they had no bodies matching Journey's description, the two women shared a breath of relief, even though the shadow of death still loomed.

Nyomi sat on the couch, clutching a cushion to her chest like it was her only lifeline.

"I don't know what else to do," she whispered, her voice cracked with exhaustion.

Cybil glanced through the window just in time to see Hayden pull up in the driveway. She and Nyomi jumped to the door, hope flickering in their eyes, thinking maybe, just maybe, Hayden had good news. Cybil yanked the door open, but the look on his face killed their hope on the spot.

"What's wrong?" Nyomi demanded, her heart already sinking.

Hayden didn't say a word. He just handed her his phone, the video already cued up. Cybil and Nyomi huddled over it, their faces tense as the footage played out. They watched the man in the video dismantle his opponents with surgical brutality. Then Nyomi's face flashed on the screen for that brief second, right beside him.

Cybil's eyes widened in disbelief, her mouth hanging open, but Nyomi's expression stayed cold, unreadable. When the video ended, she handed the phone back to Hayden with a flick of attitude.

"What's this got to do with Journey being missing'?" Nyomi's voice was sharp, guarded. "Those assholes heckled us, tried to rob us."

Hayden rubbed the back of his neck, frustrated.

"Nyomi, you don't get it. That man—he's the one who might be behind the dealer killings. If the cops tie you to him, you could be considered a suspect."

Nyomi's eyes locked onto his, hard and unflinching.

"You think I give a fuck about that? These dealers ruin lives without blinking. My daughter is still out there somewhere because of them!"

Hayden leaned in closer, his voice low, urgent.

"Taking the law into his own hands ain't the way. People are dead, Nyomi. If you keep rollin' with him, you're gonna get caught up. He's gonna get himself lit, and I don't know how close you are to him, but you need to fall back before it's too late. Let the system handle this."

Nyomi's laugh was bitter, like she'd been waiting for this moment to say what was really on her mind.

"The system? That system already failed me, Hayden. Journey's out there somewhere, maybe worse off than dead, and what's the system doing? You're sitting here on administrative leave because your partner killed a young black man, and we supposed to just hope it works itself out?"

She stepped closer, her voice dropping to a near whisper, but the intensity in her words was sharp enough to cut.

"I don't care about those fucking dealers. If someone's makin' them pay, good. If that man can help me find Journey, I'll back him all the way, whether you're with me or not."

Hayden stared at her, stunned by the fire in her words.

Cybil, standing quietly this whole time, suddenly spoke up.

"So what's the move, then? If we're gonna do this, now's the time."

Hayden glanced between the two women, feeling the weight of their determination pressing down on him. The badge he used to wear, the one that gave him purpose, felt like a distant memory now. The thrill of the chase was back, creeping into his soul like an old addiction, tempting him with possibilities he shouldn't be considering.

He rubbed his chin, thinking hard, trying to make sense of it all.

"Maybe meeting him ain't such a bad idea," he murmured, the words slipping out before he could stop them. He knew he was treading dangerous ground, but the idea of riding with the vigilante instead of against him sparked something he hadn't felt in a long time. And right now, with Nyomi's intensity burning in his mind, it didn't seem like such a crazy idea.

36

Laughter and moans seeped through thin, patchwork curtains in each cramped room. Men with eyes averted, collars turned up, shuffled along the threadbare carpet. Women in tattered gowns, toothy smiles stretched wide, leaned against peeling wallpaper, scanning the hall for the next weary soul, someone looking to lose themselves in the musky, stifling air that soaked every corner of the place. Construction was rattling up on the roof, but it didn't stop business. Nothing ever did.

Floyd's broad shoulders cut through the dimly lit corridor of the brothel, taking a break from that brutal sun beating down on him up top. Ivan's eyes tracked him until two Latino women floated by in see-through lingerie, dark, puffy nipples daring every man in sight. Floyd felt their eyes on him, too, but he kept moving. He knew the whole place was under surveillance; Ivan didn't need to hover.

Minutes passed, and break was over. Floyd slipped back into line, almost robotic, like the other workers, until he spotted Katia, slipping out of a room with some John on her arm. His breath got caught in his throat. The door behind her hung open for just a second too long. Perspiration dotted his forehead; his heart raced. This could be his death sentence, sneaking away, but he was beyond thinking of consequences. He paused outside a door, hearing soft sobs drift through. Steeling himself, he slipped in, closing it quietly behind him. Katia sat there, eyes hollow, despair dragging her down. The sight hit him like a punch.

"You Benji's cousin?" he whispered, voice low, a mix of strength and a touch of something that'd been buried a long time. She looked up, a flicker of disbelief cutting through the pain. Before she could speak, Floyd pressed a finger to his lips, quick.

"I'm coming to get you," he said, voice steady, the promise solid. "Be ready. We're getting out of here."

A faint glimmer sparked in her eyes, a shred of hope cutting through the darkness. No words needed, just the understanding. Together, they'd fight their way out. The hell they'd been trapped in was coming to an end.

37

Reginald's car crept through the damp streets of Waterbury, its engine a low growl slicing through the stillness of the night. His bloodshot eyes, heavy-lidded and bleary, scanned the streets, hunting for the martial artist—the mark on this dark mission. A near-empty bottle hung from his fingertips, the last swig of liquid courage burning his gut. Around him, street dudes hugged the block, exchanging secrets of the hit, whispers drifting through hungry hands about the bounty on the martial artist's head.

Scenes of marital battles twisted in Reginald's mind—a relentless reel of arguments, accusations, and unmet needs, feeding his reckless edge. The once-clear lines between right and wrong now blurred into the city's dark web. Tonight, he was just another goon, grinding for a come-up, hoping his Glock would settle the score with the martial artist. The murder and mayhem he'd set off might be the cap on his career, but the reward on Marcel's head called to him like salvation.

The dim dashboard lights cast an eerie glow across his

face, deepening the harsh lines of anger and exhaustion. The consequences—jail time, losing his job, a definite divorce—seemed distant now, stripped of meaning in the face of the hunt. Reginald was a man severed from the life he once had, a man on a collision course with nothing left to lose.

38

In a rundown bar on the outskirts of town, where the stale scent of old beer mixed with the tang of cigarette smoke, Richard leaned closer, eyes locked on the young blue-eyed blonde across from him. The flickering neon light from the "open" sign cast an eerie glow over her face, highlighting the playful smirk dancing on her lips. She toyed with a stray curl, leaning in with a sultry whisper over the haze of drunken laughter around them.

"You know, I could show you a night you won't forget," she teased, tracing the rim of her glass with a slender finger. "For the right price, of course."

Richard's smile was all charm, but his eyes stayed cold, predatory. He nodded, feigning interest as he asked about her rates, his words slipping out easy, calculated. Behind that mask, his mind churned with sick, dirty thoughts.

...

In the dope fiend infested hotel, the hooker stood behind Richard as he fumbled with his key, pushing it into the lock. The room was musty and hot, tucked away from ear hustlers and nosy neighbors. He'd chosen the spot knowing his deeds could stay hidden here. In his mind, he planned it all—the beatings, the choking, the final moments before packing her body up for some desert memorial he wouldn't lose a wink of sleep over.

The woman leaned against the wall, texting, her silhouette sharp against the faint light. Richard glanced over, feeling the sweat trickle down his face, his urge to kill coiling tight inside him. She looked young, maybe nineteen, twenty tops. Vulnerable, yet when he stepped closer, he noticed something different—her eyes held a steely resolve he hadn't caught back at the bar.

"Got something special for you tonight," she whispered, her voice husky, holding a hidden threat.

He smirked, moving closer, lust thick in his blood, his urges swelling with every step. That's when the shadows shifted. Another figure slid out of the darkness; the cold glint of a gun aimed square at his chest. Richard froze, his mind catching somewhere between a plea and a curse, as the unknown assailant stepped forward. The hooker's hand moved fast, pulling something from his pocket—his own switchblade, now in her grip.

"Game's over," she said, her voice calm, steady. The last thing Richard heard was the dull thud of his heartbeat, then the sharp crack of the gun. His body jerked once before slumping to the piss-stained beige carpet, blood pooling around him, mixing with the grime.

The blonde looked down, smiling devilishly at his lifeless, open-eyed stare. But her victory was short-lived. Gus moved in fast, turning his cannon on her and blasting a hole clean through her petite frame, ending her right where she stood.

As Gus was leaving, he thought of the anguish that would twist Lulu's face once she found out her twisted foster brother was gone. He didn't care. Sloan was his boss, and in this game, you did what you were told—or you'd be transitioning to whatever afterlife waited for you.

39

The cold concrete of the bunker pressed against Floyd's bare feet as Ivan held a steady grip on his handgun, shoving him toward the bathroom. Other guards lounged around, trading nasty jokes and swapping war stories, laughing loud enough for their voices to bounce off the bunker walls. They didn't see the tension simmering between Floyd and his captor. They didn't care.

Floyd shuffled forward, the barrel of Ivan's gun pressed tight against his back, a reminder of the violence one twitch away. When they reached the bathroom, Ivan shoved him inside hard. Floyd stumbled but kept himself upright, heading for the urinal, heart hammering as he played up a struggle with his zipper. Ivan kept creeping closer, watching him like a hawk, gun still in hand. Then, fate stepped in; Ivan lost his grip, and the gun clattered to the floor. In that moment, Floyd moved, lunging for the weapon, and Ivan scrambled too. They locked in a messy, brutal fight, hands and elbows flying until Floyd's fingers wrapped around the cold metal of the gun. In one swift move, he jammed the barrel against Ivan's forehead.

"Move and I'll shoot your fuckin' ass," Floyd growled, voice flat and sure. Ivan's eyes went wide, hands lifting up in surrender. Floyd grabbed him by the neck and muscled him back through the bunker, his eyes flicking left and right, keeping the gun steady against Ivan's temple. The other guards kept laughing, oblivious to the scene unfolding.

When they reached the outside, the desert stretched out in front of them, cold and dark, under a black, starless sky. Floyd forced Ivan to hand over his keys and phone.

"You're make big mistake. You know who you fucking with, da?" Ivan muttered, his voice dripping with hate.

Ignoring him, Floyd smashed the gun across his head, over and over, until Ivan lay still, broken on the ground. Floyd pocketed the keys and the phone, then slipped into Ivan's assigned Hummer, gunning the engine as he peeled off. He pulled up the emails and messages on the guard's phone, finding details of Katia's "assignment" with some politician at a nearby hotel. His fingers dug around the glove compartment, scrambling for anything that might help, and then he glanced at the dashboard. Las Vegas was fifteen miles away, but the gas light blinked at him. Cursing under his breath, Floyd figured he'd be lucky to get halfway there. But luck was all he had left to play.

...

Katia's eyes were hard, anger sparking underneath the fear as she faced down Senator Frank Spivey. The air in the room was thick with his cologne, choking her, mixing with the stale, musty smell of his armpits. Sloan's threats rang in her head, locking her in place like chains, but something inside her snapped as she looked at Spivey, his flabby skin hanging off him like rotted fruit. With a flash of disgust, she slapped him hard, her spit catching his face as her hand swung. Chaos erupted. Spivey's face turned beet red, veins bulging as he let out a roar.

"You goddamn bitch!" He lunged, his hands like steel traps, throwing her hard against the wall.

Her body hit with a sick crack, her breath hitching as he yanked her up and threw her again. Punches rained down; stomps followed. The room blurred, her vision dimming, but her spirit still burned, defiant. Then, a knock on the door sliced through the violence.

"Senator, your wife-she's ... it's serious," a strained voice called out.

Spivey stopped, his chest heaving, his eyes flicking to the door. He straightened, pulling his suit back into place as he reached for the handle. His hand shook for a second, a flicker of something that looked almost like hesitation.

The door opened, and in a heartbeat, a figure stormed in like a freight train of rage. Spivey staggered back, his face slack with shock as Floyd barreled past him. Without a second's pause, Floyd swung the gun, connecting it with Spivey's temple with a brutal thud. The senator stumbled, his head crashing against the edge of the coffee table before he crumpled, limp and useless. Floyd crossed to Katia, reaching a hand down, helping her up gently. Their eyes locked; a moment of relief and urgency passed between them.

"We gotta go, now. It's only a matter of time before someone notices him missing," Floyd said, nodding toward Spivey's sprawled form.

Katia's face flooded with confusion, gratitude, fear all at once, her voice barely a whisper.

"Who ... who are you?"

"A friend of Benji's," Floyd said, not wasting time. "I'll explain later. We gotta move."

The mention of her cousin's name lit up a spark in her. She swallowed back the fear, felt hope bloom for the first time in too long. God must've finally heard her.

They navigated the mess of the room, stepping over Spivey's unconscious body, and slipped out of the hotel, moving fast. The cool desert air hit Katia's face, a breath of freedom she'd almost forgotten. Each step away from that room felt like shedding her past, one raw, jagged piece at a time.

40

The room buzzed with the clink of fine China and low hum of whispered wealth; all eyes trained on the velvet-draped stage. Journey stood in the center, her gown draping her frame but leaving her bare breasts and pubic mound exposed, her eyes steady and resigned. Each nod from the sleek, well-dressed crowd, each smug smirk, felt like a shackle tightening, binding her to this twisted spectacle.

The auctioneer, a rotund man with a voice like rolling thunder, was in his element, hands gesturing as he painted her value in bold, shameless strokes, turning her life into promises of profit.

"Now, what will I bid for this exquisite creature?" he announced, as hands flew up, numbers rolling off tongues.

From the back, an elderly man raised his paddle, slow and deliberate, his smile slicing thin. "One million," he declared, his voice steady, cutting through the room.

"Not nearly enough for such a rare beauty," countered a woman to his right, her lips curling in a predatory grin. "Two million."

Bids spun higher, each number cold and cutting, pushing her price skyward. The crowd weighed her worth in thick stacks of cash and pure, raw ambition, stripping her down under the chandeliers, layer by layer, until there was nothing left but the exposed edge of her existence.

...

Barry's call had Diego DeJesus scrambling, urgency hot under his skin as the warning hit hard. There wasn't time to waste. Diego, thirty and street smart from a lifetime in Juarez, Mexico, earned his bread handling fentanyl, grinding out a living in the city's unforgiving element. Each movement, each pinch of that deadly powder, meant survival.

Years dripped by, the days blurring into a rhythm of mixing, measuring, every step watched by the cartel's unblinking eye. He remembered the day his luck cracked wide open—sirens blaring, drowning out his niece's birthday song from the next room. His mother's face, tear-streaked, carved itself into his memory as he was cuffed and taken away. Prison had aged him, chipping at the edges of his soul, but when the chance came to start fresh in the U.S., he didn't hesitate. Barry's voice over the phone was smooth, promising.

"Just like before, Diego. But safer. You know the stakes."

The money was real, too much to pass up, even if Barry's name carried whispers of danger. Diego's older brother Pedro, who'd slipped into the States a decade ago and had been in Barry's circle for the last five years, had opened the door. Barry had a plan, and with his private jet, they pulled Diego and his top Mexican goons quietly out of Mexico. That was a month ago.

Now, as Diego packed up the last of his supplies, the calm night split wide open. One gunshot. Glass shattered, shards raining down like deadly confetti, spinning around him. The shot was precise, coming from outside, some sniper scoping him from a distance. As the world blurred, thoughts of family flickered through his mind. Then, darkness dropped, quick and heavy.

41

Sophia sighed, feeling the burn of a life that'd stalled out. She'd taken hits for not moving product—been knocked out, seen Bart and Kent get cut down right in front of her, and stared down the barrel of the same gun that silenced them. Now, church was her sanctuary. She'd left the fast life behind, spending more time with her four-year-old son, but her pockets were empty. Drug money, blood money, all dried up. She had no work lined up, and she wasn't even looking. Right now, all that mattered was God, her son, and keeping her mind steady.

Sister Ruby Jones was her rock. Short, heavyset, with brown skin and dreadlocks that fell over her shoulders, Ruby was a volunteer from the church who'd stepped in when Sophia hit rock bottom. Sister Ruby felt the change in Sophia and opened her home to her, offering shelter until she got back on her feet.

Sister Ruby's meaty hands would rise when she wanted to make a point, her dreads slipping over her shoulder as she spoke.

"God will comfort you in these trying times. You just

have to be willing to meet him halfway. God's got a strange way of handling things, but he comes through right on time. All you need is a mustard seed of faith. A mustard seed can move mountains."

Sophia leaned against the cold glass of the window, hardly hearing Ruby's words. Her eyes narrowed, catching sight of Marcel across the street. The scar on the back of her head pulsed, a hard reminder of that bloody mess on Dikeman Street. His touch, the iron grip of it, still felt burned into her skin, searing her down to the bone. Ruby kept talking, spreading the gospel, but Sophia's mind churned, the decision gnawing at her. The hit on Marcel was news that hummed in her brain, a promise of justice draped in the temptation of reward money, buzzing like a fly she couldn't swat away.

Faith had held her up this last month, the only light in a dark sea, pushing her toward forgiveness, preaching strength. She'd built this new life on that, but watching Marcel walk into his home stirred something different. Barry's number practically burned a hole in her pocket. Just one call, that's all it would take. Her conscience battled as she thought of Ruby, the nice woman who'd welcomed her, and she knew she couldn't bring that heat into Ruby's house.

Closing her eyes, a silent prayer slipped from her lips, begging for an answer to a heart torn clean in two between revenge and redemption.

42

The clean lines of Floyd's gray sweatpants were smeared with grime, dust grinding into the fabric from hours ducking through back alleys and pushing past packed streets. His white t-shirt stuck to his chest, streaked with sweat and dirt, bearing the weight of a night that had scraped at their survival. Beside him, Katia moved in silence, bare feet soft against the cold concrete, her discarded heels a faint memory. Comfort was a luxury they couldn't afford.

As they slipped between strangers, Floyd leaned in close, voice a rough whisper.

"Saw your picture once, on a 'Missing' poster on Benji's wall." He glanced down, catching the quick spark in Katia's widened eyes—a flicker of surprise, maybe hope.

"We gotta get some things—food, cash, a phone," he murmured, scanning the crowd around them. "Most importantly, we got to send Benji a kite and give him the scoop." Katia gave a tight nod, but before they could take another step, a harsh laugh sliced the night air. Three men swaggered over, eyes dark with threats and mocking sneers.

Then came the sudden roar of engines. Cars barreled into the scene, brakes screeching like a war cry, and gunfire split the night wide open. The thugs collapsed, bodies hitting the ground before they had a chance to draw breath. Floyd and Katia watched, caught in the sudden stillness left by the chaos. As the cars tore off, leaving a wake of neon glows and spinning taillights, Floyd and Katia stepped forward. Moving quickly, hands deft, they went through the pockets of the fallen men, pulling out crumpled bills, just enough to keep their way forward.

43

Benji strolled down the narrow corridor of MacDougal Walker in Enfield, Connecticut, his steps heavy against the concrete walls. The thick, stale mix of sweat and disinfectant hung in the air, barely masking the constant clang of metal doors and the murmur of inmates' voices.

"Man, you see that last hand?" he laughed, nudging his cellmate, Rico. His voice held that unmistakable Spanish accent, laced with a raw, natural swagger.

"I thought I had it, man, but Miguel pulled that ace like he had it up his sleeve."

Rico smirked, shaking his head.

"You always count him out. Miguel's got that luck."

They kept talking, the easy banter offering a rare break from the grind of prison life. As they approached Benji's cell, the reality hit harder—the cold metal bunk, the small bolted-down desk, the narrow strip of window offering just a sliver of sky. The confinement was real.

"Catch you later, hermano," Rico said, clapping him on the back as he headed to his own cell.

Benji stepped inside, the door slamming shut behind him, a harsh reminder of the walls keeping him in. He dropped onto the lower bunk, the mattress creaking under his weight. Prison life had added a few pounds to his frame, but he still looked good. His curly hair hung long, his mustache and goatee trimmed sharp.

He leaned back, letting the cold metal frame press into him as he stared at the ceiling. Seventy-five years. The number echoed, a constant weight pressing down on his mind. He was only twenty-five. By the time he'd see freedom, he'd be a hundred. He let out a slow breath, that number settling in his bones. He'd come to terms with it, made his peace, or something close to it.

Four months. That's all it took him to track down the motherfuckers who killed his pregnant wife. The loss cut deep, still fresh, a raw scar that wouldn't heal. The faces of the driver and passenger played in his mind—the panic in their eyes as he closed in on them, cornered them in that dimly lit parking lot. He'd tracked them, hunted them down with an intensity that left no room for hesitation.

A brief smile crept onto his face, remembering the satisfaction, the justice he took into his own hands. But it faded quick, replaced by something darker. The person who sent them after his girl was still out there. He was sure there were others involved, lurking around in the shadows.

The cell door clanged as a guard passed, pulling him back to the now. Anger simmered low and steady, always there, filling the empty spaces of his cell. After a few minutes of pacing, Benji sat back on his bunk, grinning as he tore open the envelope he'd been holding onto. The letter inside was neatly folded. He let himself imagine the good words it might hold, a brief taste of freedom in ink.

But as he read, the grin faded, his face hardening with

each line. His hand clenched tighter around the paper, knuckles going white. The last spark of joy drained from his eyes, replaced by something cold, calculating. As he reached the end, his jaw set like stone, and old, violent thoughts clawed their way back from the depths, ready to surface.

44

Barry leaned back in his leather chair, fingers tapping slow and steady on the polished mahogany desk. Across from him, Pedro stood with his fists clenched tight at his sides. The faint light cast harsh shadows, throwing Pedro's anger into sharp relief, every line on his face carved by rage.

"Three days, Barry. Three damn days since my brother got killed." Pedro's voice shook, barely containing the fury churning inside him. "And you did nothing. Nothing to protect him."

Barry's eyes narrowed, a cold glint in his gaze, calculating and distant.

"Pedro, you know as well as I do, it's a war out there. Everybody's a target."

Pedro moved closer, slamming his fist down on the desk, sending Barry's drink spilling over the rim.

"Diego was the best cook you had! He was family! And you threw him to the wolves."

Barry didn't flinch, just sat still with a steady gaze.

"You think I wanted this? We're all in danger. Taking

out Diego was a message to all of us. We need to be smart. Not reckless."

Pedro's lip curled, his anger twisting his face.

"Smart? Letting my brother die is what you call smart? You should have protected him."

Barry leaned forward, voice dropping to a cold, menacing tone.

"Watch your tone, Pedro. We're all just trying to survive."

Pedro's eyes blazed, his fury reaching a boiling point.

"Survive? I'll show you survival."

He turned on his heel, storming out of the room, leaving Barry behind, alone with the storm he'd just unleashed.

45

Nyomi paced the length of her living room, her fists clenching and unclenching.

"We gotta contact Marcel," she said, her voice sharp with urgency. "He's the only one who can probably find Journey."

Cybil sat on the edge of the couch; concern etched deep in her brow.

"But, Nyomi, what if he's dangerous? That fentanyl cook got shot and killed last week. What if Marcel was involved?"

Hayden leaned against the doorframe, arms crossed.

"Cybil's right. We can't be trusting a vigilante. The cops are already looking for Journey. We just gotta be patient."

"Patient?" Nyomi stopped pacing, turning to face them, eyes burning.

"It's been weeks, and the police ain't done a fucking thing! I'm not gonna sit around while my daughter's out there, God knows where."

Hayden shook his head.

"I don't like this. The news said the shooter was a sniper. What if Marcel's the one who pulled that trigger on the Mexican? We don't need to get tied up with someone like him. I was open to it, but this dude's dangerous as fuck!"

Nyomi's jaw set hard.

"I'm willing to take that risk. Journey's life is more important than anything else!" She grabbed her phone, fingers steady as she dialed.

Cybil reached out, her voice shaking.

"Nyomi, please, think about this."

"I have," Nyomi said, her tone stone-cold.

"Every damn day and night since my baby went missing. This is the only way."

She pressed the phone to her ear, blocking out their protests, waiting for Marcel to pick up.

...

Jermaine's face was a road map of purple bruises and fresh cuts, each one a mark of the pain he'd earned for crossing Nate's brother, Floyd. Marcel and Nate flanked him, a silent force that needed no words. Jermaine's eyes darted between them, desperate, broken, spitting out every piece of intel he had.

Then Marcel's phone chimed, slicing through the thick silence. He glanced down, frowning as Nyomi's name lit up on the screen—a name from the past he thought he'd never hear from again. He picked up, her voice hitting him fast and frantic, barely held together.

"My daughter is missing. I think... I think she's been taken."

A dark rage flared up in Marcel. He clenched his fist, feeling the hard line of his knuckles. Predators. He loathed them with everything he had.

"I'll help," Marcel said, his voice a cold promise.

Nyomi paused, then her voice wavered.

"There's something else. My cousin-in-law... he's a suspended cop. He wants to help."

Marcel's jaw tightened.

"I don't like working with cops," he muttered. "But I need to meet him."

46

Marcel and Nate crouched low in the thick bush, eyes locked on the mini mansion sprawled out in front of them. Barry's crib was a straight-up display of power, showing off wealth with every square inch. The lawn stretched out wide, flawless and gleaming under the moon, with foreign cars—Lamborghinis, Ferraris, even a beefed-up Rolls-Royce, lined up like trophies. Security roamed the grounds, suited up, their hands never far from heat tucked in all the right places.

Marcel's gaze swept the scene, his pulse thumping.

"I saw her," he murmured, almost to himself. "The girl from Dikeman Street."

Seeing Sophia was a punch to his gut, reminding him just how deep he was getting. His cover hung by a thread now, and with Nyomi's daughter tangled up in this shit, the stakes hit the ceiling.

Nate's eyes narrowed, tracking where Marcel's focus had gone. His jaw clenched, fingers gripping his binoculars a little tighter. He didn't flinch, didn't ask; he just observed Marcel's reaction like he was reading between the lines.

"She spot you?" Nate's voice was flat, like he didn't expect an answer he'd have to think too hard on.

Marcel shook his head. "I don't know, but we got to be smart. Fast and invisible. Any slip here, and it's over."

Nate drew a long breath, didn't break his stare.

"I'll silence her," he said, dead calm, like he'd already made his peace with it.

Marcel turned, his face unreadable, steady, but his eyes saw more than Nate's words. He recognized that hunger to prove something, the sharp edge that came with inexperience. Nate was walking a line he'd seen plenty cross, a line he'd crossed himself when he didn't know better.

Marcel let Nate's words hang between them, heavy in the night air. Then he spoke, his tone cold and low.

"I killed an innocent woman once, Nate. She had nothing to do with any of this—just happened to be where she shouldn't. Wrong place, wrong time."

Marcel's eyes shifted, the shadows in them deep, haunted.

"You don't want to carry that. It don't go away, no matter how you try to shake it. Believe that."

The words settled, sharp and undeniable. Marcel's voice held hard-won wisdom; a warning wrapped in cold steel. He hoped it would cut through Nate's bravado, make him think twice before stepping where there'd be no turning back.

As they stayed in that heavy silence, Nate's phone buzzed. It was his aunt Gladys. Late as it was, the call itself seemed out of place. He answered, expecting anything but the voice that hit his ears next. His brother. Floyd's voice, clear as day. Nate's breath caught, his expression shifting. A flood of emotion washed over him, a flash of disbelief giving way to a slow, widening smile that broke through the tension. His eyes shimmered, his whole face softened, lighting up like he'd been pulled out of the shadows.

Floyd was alive.

47

The new strip club in Stamford, Connecticut that Barry built last year was alive, neon lights slicing through the smoke-filled air, casting twisted colors over the packed room. The bass was pounding, thumping through chests, blending into the rhythm of sweaty bodies pressed tight, dollar bills waving under the bright, hot lights. Strippers twirled and slid, their skin gleaming, pulling every eye in the room toward them, while the men leaned in close, drinks in hand, cash flashing, hungry.

This was Barry's spot—his cash cow, his fortress. He ran it like a machine, one that never slowed down, never needed sleep. The place reeked of perfume, sweat, and booze. Laughter and wild shouts clashed against the bass, filling every corner, shutting out the world outside. This club was its own world, and Barry was king here.

But then, like a slap in the face, the mood snapped. The doors burst open, and three men walked in like they owned the joint. Pedro was upfront, cutting a path, flanked by two Mexican stone-faced men at his side. The music kept blasting, but an icy ripple slid through the crowd, heads turning, tension thickening in the air.

Pedro didn't waste a second, just lifted his arm, the glint of a pistol in his hand. For a breath, silence fell, just the beat still pounding in the background. Then, gunshots ripped through the ceiling, plaster showering down. Screams tore out as tables flipped, glass shattered, and strippers bolted from the stage, heels slamming against the floor in a scramble to escape.

Panic exploded like wildfire. People rushed, chairs toppled, broken glass scattered. Bodies jammed toward exits, clawing, pushing, desperate to get free. But Pedro's men stood their ground, blocking, keeping it contained. No one got hurt, but the message was unmistakable. Barry's untouchable grip on the place wasn't as solid as he thought.

As the last shot echoed, Pedro holstered back his gun, eyes sweeping over the wreckage, the mess of his warning left behind.

"This is just the beginning," he murmured, then spun around, leading his crew out the door. Behind them, the club lay in ruins, a promise of what was to come hanging heavy in the air.

48

The sky darkened as thick clouds gathered overhead, swirling like the promise of chaos. A sudden flash of blinding light split the heavens, followed by a deafening roar that shook the ground hard enough to rattle windows in their frames. Fierce winds whipped the trees, bending them under the storm's wrath. Each strike of lightning bathed the landscape in a ghostly white glow, a cold, haunting light that cut through the Brass City.

Hayden moved slow, strutting across the debris-strewn, grime-ridden floor of the abandoned factory. Rats, bats, birds, and mice scurried around the place like it was their personal playground, but none of that fazed Hayden more than the trouble he knew he'd be facing with Nyomi. Then a dog's bark echoed in the distance, making Hayden pause. He'd been told to turn in all his firearms. He did, except for one. As soon as Hayden's fingers brushed the handle of his Sig, a red dot settled on his hand.

Marcel's voice cut through the tension like a blade.

"I don't know you, and I won't disrespect you by

putting this dot on your head, but I will blow your dominant hand off if you don't get it away from that gun."

Hayden's hand slowly moved away from his Sig Sauer. He couldn't see Marcel in the dark, but the threat came through loud and clear. As Hayden's body stiffened, Marcel whistled, a rhythm that called a now healthy Chinese Shar-Pei to his side. The dog sniffed Hayden's hand and leg, judging him for itself before returning to Marcel's side. When the next flash of lightning lit up the factory, Hayden got a good look at Marcel, Beam, and a man who looked like he'd had every inch of information and memory beaten right out of him. Hayden let out a low gasp.

Marcel's tone stayed easy.

"If you came in peace, I'm all about peace."

He flicked the switch on a plastic lantern, casting a bright light over the scene. Now Hayden could see the bruises, cuts, and swelling on the man's face, the work of Marcel and Nate's handiwork.

Hayden nodded, his eyes locked on the mess of a man in front of him.

"Did he come in peace?"

Marcel shook his head.

"No."

With calm precision, he screwed a silencer onto his gun, aimed in one swift motion, squeezed the trigger, and made Jermaine a memory in the silence that followed.

"What the...."

"So I still can't trust you?" Marcel's voice stayed ice-cold, the gun now trained on Hayden's chest, smoke still curling from the barrel.

"You leave me no fucking choice," Hayden muttered, turning away from the mess of a man he now had to work with, tension thick in every step.

49

Marcel stood dead center in Nyomi's cozy living room, his presence like an anchor, pulling every eye to him. Nate leaned against the doorway, arms crossed tight, a hard look on his face. Houston and Beam, Marcel's dogs, sat at Nate's feet, eyes sharp, ears perked, like they knew something heavy was about to go down.

Nyomi, perched on the edge of the couch, a mix of grit and worry across her face. She looked over at Nate, catching that rare glimmer in his eyes when he found out his brother Floyd was still alive. That flash of joy made her feel a spark of hope she hadn't felt in a minute.

Marcel's voice cut through the room, steady and raw.

"Next phase is straight up but serious. Nate, you're driving Nyomi and the dogs to Nevada. Don't take it the wrong way, Nyomi, but Journey might be out there. It's dangerous, but it's our only shot."

Nyomi's brow tightened, leaning forward.

"Why can't we just fly? We'd get there faster."

Marcel shook his head, cold and clear.

"I don't want your name on anything official. If things fall apart when we go after Journey, your names clean. Same goes for you, Nate."

Nate nodded, understanding exactly where Marcel was coming from.

"Got it. We'll be ready to roll soon as we can."

Nyomi exhaled, that hint of tension loosening.

"Alright. I'll start packing."

Marcel gave a quick nod, then turned toward the door.

"I'll link up with Hayden. We need to meet before this goes any deeper. Not sure about your pig boy, but for Journey's sake, I'm keeping an open mind. Ny..."

"I got it, Marcel," Nyomi replied, her voice low, serious. She caught Marcel's drift.

As Marcel stepped out, Nyomi got up and headed to her bedroom, her mind already running through what she'd need to take. Nate crouched down, gave Houston and Beam a firm pat, then grabbed their leashes.

"We need you two on your best behavior," he muttered to the dogs. They looked up at him, tails wagging, ready for whatever lay ahead.

With everyone locked in their own tasks, silence settled over the room, thick with purpose. The clock was ticking, each second bringing them closer to a showdown they all knew had to happen.

...

In Hartford, Barry stood back, shrouded in the darkness of the alley, his eyes fixed on Pedro's car parked along Park Avenue in Hartford. His heart thumped steady and hard, a rhythm honed by the hours he'd spent watching and planning. The two goons leaned against the car, relaxed, oblivious, laughing like they had the world in their hands. They had no idea they were moments away from hell. Barry's thumb hovered over the detonator; his whisper lost in the night air.

"See you in hell."

One firm press, and the explosion shattered the quiet. Fire swallowed the car in a single, vicious breath, turning it into a furnace of flames and smoke. Debris shot through the air, tearing across the street, rattling windows, and triggering car alarms up and down the block. The fire lit the night in a flash of revenge, burning hot and bright.

Barry didn't linger. He knew the blast would bring all kinds of heat, and he couldn't afford to get caught. Slipping into the dark night, his thoughts turned to his next move. Jermaine. With Pedro and his crew wiped off the map, the path was clear. Barry's mind sharpened, relentless. The vigilante always seemed to stay a step ahead, but that was about to change. The hunt pressed on, and Barry wouldn't stop until he'd settled every score.

50

Detective Lewis leaned against the water cooler, his brow furrowed, deep in thought.

"You hear about Sharpe," he said, his voice low and steady.

Officer Daniels glanced around, cautious.

"Yeah, I heard. Administrative leave and then jailed. That fucker is up shit's creek."

Lewis shook his head, an edge of disdain in his voice.

"And now he's trying to cash in on that hit the drug lord put out on the vigilante. Can you believe that shit?"

Daniels scoffed, eyes narrowing.

"The guy always had a knack for making a fucked up situation worse."

Lewis sighed, hardening his tone.

"Some people just never change. Even when they're down and out, they find a way to dig deeper."

Around the corner, Officer Cyr listened intently, his ears tuned to every word about Reginald Sharpe. Each word sharpened his focus, sinking in.

"Trying to cash in on a hit, huh," Cyr muttered, his mind spinning with possibilities.

Without hesitation, he slipped out of the station, his steps quick and tight with purpose. Outside, he snatched his phone, fingers trembling with urgency as he dialed Hayden.

"Hayden, it's Cyr. You're not going to believe what I just heard..."

...

Hayden's phone buzzed, and he glanced at the screen, spotting Cyr's name. Picking up, he absorbed every word, each detail dropping like a stone in his gut. Reginald was hunting—and the target was Marcel.

Hayden pushed to his feet, the chair scraping the floor, tension rippling through his stance. Reginald was relentless, like a bloodhound with a scent. Glancing at the clock on the wall, he knew there was no time to spare. The memory of Marcel putting down Jermaine resurfaced, and Hayden felt that grip around his throat. Marcel had him by the balls, and stepping out of line meant certain death.

Grabbing his jacket, he felt the weight of the choice bearing down. Marcel needed this intel, plain and simple. Walking blind into Reginald's trap meant the game was over. With Journey's fate nudging him forward, he grabbed his keys, his jaw clenched in resolve. Time to act, no turning back.

51

The intruders slid into Marcel's apartment, tension so thick it could choke a man. Three of them, moving cautious, eyes cutting through the dimly lit room like they knew a ghost lurked in those shadows. Floorboards creaked, and their hearts pounded faster, the knowledge of who they were up against thrumming in their veins. But mission confidence pushed them forward, steeling their nerves.

Then Marcel appeared, moving like a ghost in the night. One second, the goon was there, next second, he felt the blade's cold kiss against his throat. The other two froze, guns still in their hands, disbelief and fear plain on their faces.

"Drop them," Marcel's voice, a deadly whisper, left no room for thought. Their eyes darted between their cornered buddy and Marcel's .380 aimed their way. Weapons hit the floor, clattering in surrender.

Marcel's gaze held an icy rage as he tightened his grip, and with one swift motion, the first goon's throat split under the blade. He dropped, lifeless before he hit the ground. The .380 spoke next, two muffled shots sending the second man sprawling, his stare gone blank. The last one, pale and trembling, got forced to his knees, Marcel leaning in, breath hot against his ear.

"Call your boss," he growled. "Tell him we caught Marcel slipping. We're running out the back now. Now blow this bitch up. But while you're at it, who were your buddies?"

...

Lil' George sat behind the wheel, pocked face flushed, pale skin stretched thin over adrenaline fueled excitement. He was high on the idea of that payday, six figures flashing before his eyes. Hands trembling, he struck a match, lighting the first Molotov cocktail. With a fierce toss, the bottle shattered against the three-family house's side, flames exploding, climbing hungrily. His breath quickened, lit the next one, launched it harder. A third followed, each burst stoking his frenzy. He didn't feel the tears on his face, didn't hear the screams of anguish inside. His mind locked on that money, greed blinding him.

In his head, the vigilante lay charred inside. Marcel's greatest con-Lil George's own greed feeding him lies. Minutes later, the blaze swallowed the building whole.

52

Officer Cyr stepped onto the charred remains on Albert Place with Officers Reynolds and Thompson. They moved through the chaos, their routine practiced and cold. The flames were finally snuffed out, leaving a smoking skeleton where a three-family home once stood. Yellow tape cut off the area from the curious, while firefighters and forensic teams sifted through the wreckage under the unforgiving glare of the spotlights.

"This was Bailey Moore's place," a detective muttered to Cyr as they approached what was left. The weight of the words hit hard. The vibrant life that once lived here was now nothing but ashes and twisted metal, the remains of a home swallowed by fire.

Cyr's gaze fell on the charred bodies, their outlines barely hidden beneath the white sheets covering them, a stark reminder of what the fire had claimed. The stench of burnt wood and flesh clung to the air, sharp and nauseating, a bitter trace of the night's horror.

While they documented the scene, Cyr's unease thickened, his thoughts snagging on whispers he'd heard earlier that week about suspended Officer Sharpe. Suspended or not, Sharpe's name seemed to keep finding its way into the mix, linked to cases he shouldn't have been anywhere near. People had been talking, sharing quiet accusations behind closed doors, hinting he knew more than he let on. Some had even said they'd seen him in places that made no sense for an officer on leave.

Cyr tried to shove it aside, tried to zero in on the work in front of him. But his mind kept drifting back. The scene here, the stories about Sharpe, it was like pieces of a puzzle that didn't quite fit but somehow felt connected. The night stretched on, thick with smoke and unanswered tension, and a part of Cyr couldn't shake the feeling this fire wasn't just an accident.

53

The dense canopy of the Chequamegon-Nicolet National Forest cast shadows as thick as tar over the clearing, where three men, looking more beast than human, stood watch. Hidden deep in Wisconsin's rural wilds, the clearing was a fortress of towering pines and tangled underbrush, cut off from prying eyes. Six kids huddled together, eyes wide, breath tight with fear as they waited for whatever fate had in store.

Lenny, the leader, looked like he'd spent more time in the forest than out of it. A scraggly beard streaked with gray covered his scarred, weather-beaten face. His sharp, calculating eyes constantly scanned the edges of the clearing. A tattered flannel shirt clung to his wiry frame, sleeves rolled up over forearms marked with old tattoos and fresh scratches from the woods. Mud and grease stained his loose jeans, a fitting second skin.

Beside him, Joe hunched over, his greasy hair falling in clumps around a face pale as death, dirt caked under his nails, and his scowling lips twisted to reveal teeth yellowed and worn down. His clothes barely held together, a mess of worn-out rags that looked ready to fall off him. An old hunting knife hung at his belt, the blade chipped and rusted.

The third man, Hank, loomed like a mountain. Towering over the other two, he was a shadow of raw muscle and menace, his face an emotionless mask broken by a badly healed nose and eyes that seemed set too close together. His tangled hair was tied back, and a sleeveless vest over his filthy shirt showed arms thick with muscle, crude tattoos scratched into his skin.

The kids, dirty and worn, clung to each other, breaths shallow. The oldest, a boy barely twelve, tried to shield the younger ones, his eyes flicking between the men and the thick woods, desperate for any way out.

Lenny grunted, breaking the tense quiet.

"They shoulda been here by now," he muttered, voice a rough scrape. He spat, the dark glob landing near Joe's boots.

Joe shifted, fingers twitching toward the knife at his waist.

"Maybe they got held up. Cops been nosin' around lately."

Hank stepped forward, eyes on the children, his sheer presence making the youngest girl whimper, shrinking back.

"Ain't nobody coming to save you," he growled, low and mean.

Lenny shot him a hard look.

"Ease up, Hank. Don't need 'em scared outta their wits. Not yet."

The forest seemed to hold its breath; the usual sounds of wildlife muted. A breeze stirred, bringing the sharp scent of pine and earth. Overhead, the sky darkened toward night.

Lenny glanced at his battered, cracked watch.

"Another hour," he said to no one in particular. "If they ain't here, we're movin'."

Joe gave a tight nod, worry flickering in his eyes.

"They better bring the right payment. Last thing we need is a screw-up."

Hank's lip curled in a nasty smile.

"We'll get ours. One way or another."

Lenny let his phone chime a few times before he picked up.

"Dominic, tell me you're pullin'... wait, what? Two fuckin' days?"

His teeth ground together, fingers gripping the phone. The truck, supposed to take the kids, had broken down and was fixed, but instead of risking it again, the higher-ups postponed the pickup until a new truck was ready, in two days. Lenny's face went redder as he listened, his fist clenched like he wanted to smash the phone but stopped himself. No good could come from that.

While Lenny cursed at the messenger, Joe and Hank went still, hearing a heavy thud somewhere in the woods. Lenny heard it too, snapping his phone shut. The men moved slowly toward the sound, each step cautious.

...

Nate's heart thundered, adrenaline pumping hard. Tonight, he'd gather the intel Marcel wanted. After Nyomi had dozed off with the dogs, Nate slipped out of bed, careful not to wake her. Marcel made it clear: Nyomi didn't need to know about any of this, especially tonight's mission. The less she knew, the safer she was.

Nate parked a mile out, moving with a silent precision through the pitch-black woods. He crept closer to the clearing, low voices drifting through the dark. Crouching behind an oak, he peered into the scene. The hillbillies matched Jermaine's description—rough, mean, and ready for anything. The campfire flickered, throwing twisted shadows on their faces.

Lenny's voice carried, low and gravelly. "They better show up soon," he said, glancing around. Nate noted how Lenny moved—always alert, never resting.

Joe was pacing, his greasy hair catching the firelight. His hand twitched near his knife, his gaze shifting toward the trail leading out.

"This don't feel right," he muttered. "We're sittin' ducks out here."

Hank stood silent; eyes glued to the kids. The sight of them huddled in fear twisted something in Nate's gut.

Nate scanned the clearing. A rusted pickup sat parked with old crates piled in the back. The kids were tied up, ropes thick around their wrists, trapped in a rough circle of logs and branches. A tattered tent flapped in the breeze, supplies visible inside—food, water, a couple of sleeping bags.

He studied the setup, taking in the hillbillies' weapons. Lenny had a shotgun slung over his shoulder; Joe kept his knife within reach, and Hank had size and brute strength on his side.

Creeping closer, Nate shifted his foot—and his boot snapped a dry leaf.

Hank's head whipped around. "Did you hear that?"

His hand went to his gun. Lenny snapped his phone shut; Joe nodded, signaling for Hank to follow him.

Nate pressed himself flat against the ground, Glock tight in his sweaty grip. The two men came toward him, eyes searching the underbrush, the crunch of leaves underfoot growing louder. Hank's breath puffed white in the cold night air, steady as a machine. Joe's fingers twitched near his knife, gaze darting from shadow to shadow.

Hank nudged a pile of leaves with his boot.

"Probably an animal," he grunted.

Joe's shoulders relaxed.

"Let's go back. We ain't got time to chase ghosts."

They turned, still cautious but easing up. Nate stayed motionless, every nerve alive, as they drifted back toward the clearing, shadows stretching long behind them. When they were far enough, he shifted just enough to ease the pressure off his knees, ready for whatever came next.

54

Hayden stood near the window, his back turned to Cybil, who was sitting stiffly on the edge of the bed, arms crossed tight over her chest. The first light of dawn pushed through the curtains, painting a pale glow over faces worn from tension.

"You're on administrative leave, and now you're about to drive cross-country with a murderer. What the fuck, Hayden?" Cybil's voice shook, the edge between anger and desperation sharp as glass.

"A whim, Hayden, a damn whim. Taking a chance like that. I can't believe I let Nyomi talk you into this suicide mission."

Hayden clenched his fists, his gaze fixed on the city outside, forcing himself to block out the memory of Marcel ending Jermaine without a blink. "I gotta go, Cybil. Marcel needs me. We got a lead, and it might be the only shot."

Cybil's eyes followed him as he stuffed clothes, guns, ammo, and a few other essentials into a bag. She could see it was pointless to argue; his mind was made. He was locked in.

As the door shut behind him, Cybil slumped onto the couch, shoulders wracked with silent sobs. She knew he had to go, but the fear of losing him was like a knife twisting in her gut. And now, with Journey either dead or lost to the brutal world of human trafficking, the weight was almost unbearable.

55

Captain Lark stood at the front of the roll call room, face like stone, a mix of command and pain etched across it. The usual buzz of pre-shift chatter was gone, replaced by a silence that felt thicker than concrete. Lark's voice, usually sharp and loud, was a low, steady current, cutting through the tension as he began.

"Tragedy struck last night," he said, eyes scanning the room of officers, faces hardened and tense.

"Officer Reginald Sharpe and former officer Brian Kite were found burned alive in a house on Albert Street."

The shock hit the room like a punch, a ripple of gasps and murmurs filling the air.

Lark let it settle, then pushed on.

"Officer Sharpe served this department with dedication, even if he'd been tangled up in some controversy lately. He was still one of ours."

His gaze grew colder.

"And Kite, yeah, disgraced and dismissed, but still a

piece of this department's history. Regardless of their paths, their deaths are a blow to us all."

The captain's tone shifted, rougher now, steering them into darker waters.

"We also got a report—a girl gone missing right across the street from where the fire went down. Same time. This could mean something bigger."

The room hung heavy with unspoken words, grief, suspicion, a raw mix of confusion and loss. Officers cast glances around, heads shaking, low whispers slipping through clenched teeth. Some hugged, others clasped shoulders in silent solidarity, their bond tightening in the face of shared pain.

Officer Cyr, leaning against the back wall, felt a chill of grim satisfaction slide through him. He knew, just like a few others did, that Sharpe was in deep with some dark shit. And Kite, well, nobody was shocked to hear he'd gone out the way he had. Cyr discreetly pulled out his phone, firing off a text to Hayden, knowing he'd want to hear this right away.

When Lark finally wrapped up, the weight of his last words sank in, lingering in the stale air. Cyr dialed Hayden's number right after, dropping the news on him about Officer Sharpe's end.

...

Over at Barcelo Aruba, Christina was stretched out on a lounge chair by the pool, sun catching her auburn hair, her laughter floating out as Madison cracked a joke. The day felt miles away from the chaos back home. Christina's phone buzzed, and she glanced down at it, her smile easing.

"Who now?" Madison teased, sipping her iced tea.

"Just an update from the center," Christina replied. "They finally found a foster home for the Thompson twins. You remember them—the ones from that nightmare last month?"

Madison's eyes softened, respect plain on her face.

"You're a miracle worker, you know that? Those kids worship you."

Christina just shrugged, a hint of color touching her cheeks.

"I just do what I can. Those kids deserve something better."

Madison reached out, gave Christina's hand a quick squeeze.

"You gave them that shot. You're a hero, Chris."

Christina's gaze drifted over the pool, her thoughts slipping miles away.

"Wish I could do more."

56

arcel crouched low behind the worn sofa, every muscle in his teenage body taut, every instinct screaming to stay hidden. The stench of sweat and fear thickened the air, blending with the faint scent of blood seeping into the old carpet. Buddy stood in the center of the room, chest heaving from the fight. The gun in his hand smoked faintly, the sharp crack of gunfire that had rocked the small house now replaced by an eerie silence. But it wasn't just the gun that had done the damage.

The first guy thought he could take Buddy down with brute force, charging like a bull. But Buddy was faster. Marcel had watched, wide-eyed, as Buddy sidestepped the attack like it was nothing, driving his knee into the thug's stomach with bone-crushing force. The man doubled over, and Buddy's elbow slammed down on the back of his neck, sending him crumpling to the floor. The second one thought he was smarter, circling Buddy with fists raised, looking for an opening. But Buddy was ahead, jabbing quick to the throat. The man choked, gasping, and Buddy spun, delivering a roundhouse kick that connected with a sickening thud against the guy's temple. He hit the ground, out cold.

Buddy's girl screamed, tried to run, but the third thug grabbed her, his gun pointed at her head. Marcel caught the desperation in her eyes, a silent plea for help, but he stayed frozen. The thug yelled something, only to get cut off by the blast of Buddy's gun. The shot echoed, and the thug jerked, hitting the floor with the girl he dragged down lifeless beside him. It was either Melissa or Marcel; Buddy chose Marcel. Three bodies lay scattered across the room, blood darkening the floorboards. Buddy, breathing heavy but calm, looked down at the mess with a cold indifference. He wiped the gun clean with a rag, precise, methodical.

Marcel stayed still, trying to steady his breathing, blocking out the blood, the bodies, the violence that had just ripped through the room. But Buddy's words cut through the fog of fear.

"You stay quiet about this, Marcel," Buddy said, his voice low, calm as death itself. "Or you're next."

Marcel, heart slamming in his chest, nodded quick. He knew Buddy meant it. No room for hesitation, no room for doubt. Survival meant silence.

...

" ... and when it was over, I just nodded, like I understood, like I was good with it. But I wasn't. I just wanted to survive."

Marcel's words lingered in the quiet of the car, the final pieces of his story settling heavy. The road stretched into the night, but his mind was still trapped in that room from years back, surrounded by bodies Buddy left in his wake.

Hayden gripped the wheel, his knuckles white. He hadn't spoken since Marcel started talking, the weight of that confession hitting him like a sledgehammer. He figured Marcel had been through hell, but hearing it raw, knowing the horrors he'd witnessed, changed things.

"Man, that's ... I don't even know what to say," Hayden finally managed, voice rough.

"You don't have to say anything," Marcel replied, his tone flat but holding a trace of something else-vulnerability. "I've been carrying this around for years, never told anyone. But I needed you to know because what we're doing now ... it's all part of that. It's all connected."

Hayden let out a slow breath, his mind working to absorb it all. He could feel the weight of what Marcel just shared, the rawness of it. It wasn't just a story, it was a piece of Marcel, the thing that shaped him into the man he was.

"I get it now," Hayden said, quieter, thoughtful. "Why this is so personal for you. Why you're so driven."

Marcel nodded, looking over at Hayden, his expression softer.

"It's not just about revenge or righting wrongs. It's about making sure that darkness doesn't win. That it doesn't spread."

Hayden glanced over, a shared understanding passing between them.

"And you're not alone in this. We're in it together. I've got your back, no matter what."

A small smile tugged at Marcel's lips, a hint of a bond growing stronger between them. Marcel hadn't been close to anyone since Lupe's death.

"I know you do. And I've got yours. We're going to see this through, Hayden. And good looking out on that cop info. It was taken care of in the fire."

Hayden nodded, accepting the fate of his crooked ex-partner. The car settled into a quiet, easy silence as they drove on, the weight of the past a little lighter. For the first time in a long time, they both felt a sense of peace, knowing they weren't facing this fight alone.

As the city lights faded, the road ahead looked less daunting. They had each other, and that was enough. Whatever lay ahead, they'd face it side by side, stronger together than they'd ever been apart. That tip about Sharpe being in on the hunt was the bridge that earned Marcel's trust.

57

Barry strolled down the marble hallway of his opulent mansion, the chandelier lights bouncing off polished floors like fire off steel. He neared the front door and saw Dwight leaning against the frame, tense but collected. Barry opened the door with a silent nod. Dwight stepped onto the front steps, eyes cutting through the dimly lit street.

"Everyone's on high alert," he muttered, his voice low, gravelly. "Strapped and ready. Business as usual, despite that Mexican cook getting taken out. No deaths from fentanyl since, which is good for us. Keeps the heat off, especially with his brother out."

Barry's mouth curled into a faint smile.

"That's what I like to hear."

Dwight returned the look, but it didn't quite touch his eyes.

"Yeah. Good for business."

He turned, slipping back into the night. Barry closed the door behind him, climbing back to his bedroom. The room was dim, the soft glow from a nearby lamp casting shadows across the plush carpet. On the bed, a stunning Colombian woman lay naked, her bronzed skin gleaming in the low light. She gazed up at Barry, admiration filling her dark eyes.

"You are ... how do you say ... so good under pressure," she purred, her thick accent winding through the words. "Everything you do ... so thorough. Now everyone is eating, yes?"

Barry chuckled, sliding into bed beside her, the warmth of her body pressed against his.

"That's the idea," he replied, his voice smooth, dripping confidence. She smiled, lips brushing his skin, her hands tracing the sharp lines of his body.

"You make all ... adjustments ... perfect," she whispered. Before he could respond, she kissed his chest, her lips trailing lower, her mouth wrapping around him. Barry's eyes closed, his mind slipping away, lost in the sensation.

Hours later, he woke in darkness. The Colombian woman slept beside him, her breathing soft. He slipped out of bed and walked to the bathroom, but passing the bay window, he noticed Dwight's car still parked outside. Frowning, Barry stepped into the hall, curiosity creeping in. Moving downstairs, the mansion felt haunted, too quiet. In the living room, his pulse spiked. Dwight's lifeless body slumped on the couch, next to him Jermaine, equally still, eyes fixed but empty.

Barry's mind raced, his chest tight. He turned, bolting back upstairs, heart hammering. The woman was sound asleep, blissfully ignorant of the carnage below. He thought about waking her but felt an urge to leave her untouched. Moving swiftly, he dressed and reached for his closet, his hand sliding to the .380 he always kept there. But as he opened the door, a figure lunged from the darkness.

Marcel's eyes were cold, merciless. In one quick strike, Marcel's blade slashed across Barry's neck, the cut deep, perfect. Barry's hands flew to his throat, but life slipped from him in seconds. He crumpled to the floor, his empire bleeding out beneath him.

Upstairs, the Colombian woman shifted in her sleep, sighing softly, content. Unaware of the nightmare waiting in the morning, the knock on the door, the badges, the guns, the questions. All of it coming for a crime she'd never even seen coming.

58

Marcel crouched low beside a rusted pickup, the throwaway phone cold against his ear. He kept his eyes locked on the trafficker's compound up the road. Voices floated on the night air from the cabin-a few more minutes, and he'd strike. There was no room for mistakes tonight.

"Nate," Marcel's voice was a low whisper carried through static. "I'm moving in. I need you to be my other set of eyes."

A brief pause on the other end. and then,

"Got it," Nate replied, voice steady. "What's the play?"

A grim smile touched Marcel's lips.

"I'm taking out anyone setting up the transport for those kids. Three of them are inside now, two more coming for the pickup. Keep your eyes open. Let me know if anyone else shows."

Marcel cut the line, slid the phone into his pocket and moved. Silent steps against dirt, each movement calculated, he felt the weight of his rifle, a familiar reassurance. He found his position, sighting the three men in dim light.

Three shots, three bodies hitting the ground before they even had time to react.

From the truck, a muffled scream broke the silence, but Marcel ignored it. The kids were safe for now. His attention shifted to the cabin. Inside, Hayden held Joe at gunpoint. Joe's face was wide-eyed, sweat running down his forehead. Hank stood rigid beside Joe, jaw set, a sneer edging his lips. Defiant, his shoulders squared, and no flinch in his eyes.

"Think I'm gonna spill?" Hank scoffed, voice calm and cold. "I'll die before I say a word. You got the wrong guy if you think otherwise."

Joe glanced at Hank, fear creeping into his voice.

"Hank, maybe we-"

"Shut up, Joe!" Hank barked, his gaze fixed on Marcel.

Marcel watched, feeling time slip. Hank wasn't breaking. Patience wearing thin, Marcel saw the problem clear. He gave Hayden a nod. Hayden understood, loosening his hold just enough. Marcel moved quick, closing in. His fist struck Hank's temple-precise, lethal. Hank's eyes widened, then dulled as his body dropped, dead before he hit the ground. Joe's face paled, hands trembling. He fumbled for his phone, desperation spilling over.

"Okay, okay!" He scrolled, and then Journey's picture flashed on the screen.

Hayden's reaction was immediate, his frame going taut, eyes narrowing, tension rolling off him. He stepped forward, jamming the barrel of his gun hard against Joe's forehead. Joe flinched, a pitiful whimper slipping from his mouth.

"Where is she?" Hayden's voice came out low, dangerous, more growl than question. "Where's Journey?"

Joe stuttered, eyes darting, panic rising.

"Las Vegas! I-I think! But a buyer from another country wanted her. I don't know if the deal went through. She might still be there, or-"

Marcel snatched the phone from Joe's hand, eyes scanning messages, names, locations. Taking it all in, he nodded, absorbing every detail. Joe's trembling fingers offered up the password, scribbled on a scrap of paper.

"All the info's there," Joe stammered, voice cracked with desperation.

"Please, I-" Marcel met Hayden's gaze, unyielding.

"He was part of it," Marcel said flatly. "He admitted he was in on the ring that took Journey."

That was all Hayden needed. His face hardened, fury roiling beneath the surface. Without hesitation, he pulled the trigger, a single crack echoing in the night. Joe's body slumped, blood pooling at his feet. It was Hayden's first body, and hopefully his last. Hayden expressed no emotion; just the desire to proceed with the mission.

Marcel didn't waste time. He pulled a phone out again.

"Nate," he said, voice cold and focused. "Use one of these throwaways to call the cops. Tell them where the kids are. We're done here."

With a shared, grim understanding, Marcel and Hayden moved off, leaving the scene behind. Their next stop was locked in: Las Vegas.

59

Floyd paced the motel room, throwing hard glances at the burner phone every few minutes, like he could make it ring by force of will alone. Katia sat on the bed, foot tapping out her impatience on the worn dark red carpet. They'd done everything they could; it was a waiting game now, just hoping Nate and his people would come through. Benji got the letter, but each second they spent holed up in Las Vegas felt like time they didn't have to spare.

Katia finally broke the silence, her voice a mix of skepticism and a sliver of hope she couldn't hide.

"You think your brother's really coming? Connecticut is a long way from here. Been six days."

Floyd stopped pacing, turned to face her, voice rough but steady.

"He'll show. Ain't no way he'd leave us hanging. He got people that know how to move without leaving a trail."

But even as he spoke, his own doubts crept in. Nate and his people should've been here two days ago. Still, he held onto his words like a lifeline.

Katia crossed her arms, leaning back against the headboard.

"I just...I don't like sitting here, waiting around like some target practice. Feels like we're sitting ducks, just waiting to get picked off."

"I hear you," Floyd said, sitting down on the edge of the bed beside her. "But running out there without a plan? We're done before we hit the street. Nate's crew got the skill to get us out without nobody noticing. That is what my brother told me, and I believe him. We just gotta hold tight until they get here."

Katia nodded, though doubt still flickered in her eyes.

"And your brother, he trusts these people, yeah? They won't sell us out the second they catch a break?"

Floyd's jaw set hard, irritation simmering, though he got it—she had every reason to be paranoid.

"I don't trust nobody, not completely," he admitted, voice low and tight. "But right now, we don't got the luxury to be picky. We're playing the hand we got."

Katia let out a slow breath, the tension in her shoulders easing a fraction.

"Alright. But if anything feels off, we're out. No looking back."

"Deal," Floyd agreed, his tone firm. "Eyes open, guard up, no matter what."

They settled into a quieter silence, a little lighter but still taut, both holding onto that thin thread of hope that Nate and his people would pull through before the traffickers closed in on them. It wasn't perfect, wasn't even close—but it was all they had, and for now, that'd have to be enough.

60

The air inside the abandoned slaughterhouse hung thick with the stench of blood and decay, a rank smell of death mixed with the stale scent of fear, sticking to the walls like mold. Sloan stood in the center, twisted and powerful, dressed in a dark, impeccably tailored suit that gleamed under the industrial lights. Heavy gold chains lay over his black silk shirt, his wealth worn like armor, every detail in place to scream power. Sloan had clawed his way up, and here, in this cold hellhole, he held his crown as a man to fear, a man who demanded loyalty.

Around him, his crew loomed, hard-eyed and silent, like stone walls. Sloan's gaze swept over the five men hanging upside down, each one strung up from rusted meat hooks, bodies swaying slightly, barely recognizable beneath the swollen, pulped faces and torn skin. Blood dripped from them in slow rivulets, collecting in dark, sticky pools on the tarp beneath them. One man, twitching and gasping, held onto the last threads of life, barely hanging on.

Sloan paced, the click of his polished shoes echoing

against the concrete. He lit a cigar, taking his time with it, savoring the sharp smoke that mingled with the horror around him. He let out a cloud, watching it swirl.

"Look at you," he sneered, voice low and edged with contempt. "I gave you one simple job; keep Floyd contained. Now he's gone, and I'm out half a million."

The men stayed silent, gagged and wide-eyed with terror beneath bruised and swollen lids. Sloan's gaze was cold, empty, as he crouched near the half-dead man, his voice dropping to a soft, mocking tone. "This is what failure looks like. Let one rat slip, and you all pay the price."

He straightened, flicking his cigar toward the others, rage simmering in his stance.

"Last time any of you fuck up like this. Remember who owns this game. I own you. Your lives are mine, and I'll do whatever the fuck I want with them."

Sloan took a slow drag on his cigar, flicking the ash onto the tarp where it sparked against the blood-soaked fabric. Behind him, his enforcers stood, a wall of intimidation. This was Sloan's world-a kingdom built on fear, power, and brutal control. Sloan let his words settle like a blade sinking into flesh, the silence broken only by the wet, struggling breaths of the men hanging upside down. With a small nod, he signaled one of his men, a casual command like ordering a drink. The enforcer stepped forward, pulling out a sleek, black handgun, the kind that never jammed.

The shots echoed, each one dull, final, and precise. Each bullet hit its mark, and one by one, the bodies jerked, then went limp, blood spurting briefly before pooling beneath them. No ceremony, no pause. It was work these men had done many times before-clean, efficient, without a trace of remorse.

Sloan watched as the last one stopped twitching. Blood

seeped deeper into the tarp, staining it dark, the scene playing out like a silent, deadly ritual. He flicked his cigar to the floor, the embers scattering before dying out, like the men hanging lifeless before him.

"Clean this up."

Sloan's voice was calm, indifferent. Adjusting his suit, smoothing the fine fabric as if nothing had happened, he stepped over the bloodstained tarp, each step unhurried. His silhouette faded into the shadows, leaving his men behind to erase any trace of what had gone down here. Another lesson taught in Sloan's world, a world where failure was dealt with quickly and mercy never came.

61

Lulu thought of her dead foster brother, and her fists clenched so tight her nails dug deep, making her palms bleed. The blood didn't faze her—she'd seen rivers of it. What got to her was the empty space Richard left behind, his precise, almost artistic way of erasing bodies like secrets slipping away into the night. Her mind jumped to Sloan, his paranoia creeping out in sideways glances and the way he held back words that hung in the air like a threat.

She'd known the truth the second she heard about Richard's death. No witnesses, no trail pointing to Sloan, but she didn't need proof. The way Sloan's gaze hovered on her, lingering a moment too long, the tension in his jaw when Richard's name slid into a conversation—it all spelled out what she couldn't say out loud. He'd done it. Richard's death wasn't some rival or a random hit; it was calculated, cold, a move Sloan made when he felt cornered.

Sloan had crossed a line, and Lulu knew it. Richard, twisted as he was, had been more than her foster brother; he'd been her weapon, her fixer, the dark shadow that kept their empire running. Losing him wasn't just personal; it was a blow to the business. Sloan's paranoia cost them their sharpest tool, and now she was left to patch up the holes.

Being around Sloan now felt like a tightrope walk. Lulu kept her face straight, her words smooth, hiding every trace of her suspicion. She could feel Sloan's eyes on her, sizing her up, calculating, figuring out how much she knew. Fear wasn't the issue; she'd never been afraid of him, but she understood the game. If Sloan could kill Richard, he wouldn't flinch at taking her out if he felt she was a threat.

Lulu moved through the house with a calm grace, clocking every camera, every lurking ear. She laughed at Sloan's jokes, brushed his arm when they crossed paths, and leaned into his kiss when he wanted it. But behind her eyes was a quiet promise. She wasn't going to give him the satisfaction of watching her break. Sloan had made his move; now she'd bide her time, play the part, survive in a game where one wrong move could be her last.

One day, he'd pay for it, she told herself. Until then, Lulu kept her suspicions locked up, buried so deep Sloan would never find them.

62

SOMEWHERE IN NEVADA

The sun was sinking low, stretching across the empty highway as Hayden parked the car a few miles out from the rundown gas station. Marcel sat in the passenger seat, his jaw clenched, eyes glued to the horizon like he was daring it to move. The flyer, crumpled tight in his grip, was his ticket into the sick world that stole Journey.

"You're really going in alone," Hayden said, his voice thick with that unease he couldn't shake. "It's suicide, man."

Marcel didn't flinch. Eyes still dead ahead, he replied, "It's the only way. They don't trust nobody. This recruiter thinks I'm just another hustler, hungry for a quick dollar. I'll use that."

Hayden shook his head, eyes hard.

"What if they catch on, realize you ain't no regular thug?"

"They won't," Marcel's voice cut firm. "Not if we keep to the plan. I get inside, get close to their setup, pretend I don't know any martial arts, and track down Journey's location. You and Nate keep things locked down out here."

Minutes later, headlights lit up the dusty lot at the gas station. The recruiter. Marcel turned, eyes steady on Hayden.

"Get Nyomi and the dogs to Reno, straight to the safe house. Keep quiet, keep moving."

Hayden's fingers tightened around the wheel.

"And what about you?" His voice low, carrying a bite he couldn't hide. "Walking into a snake pit with nothing but a burner in your pocket."

"I'm asking you to trust me, not like it," Marcel's gaze was all steel now. "Keep your burner phones on. Both you and Nate. Anything goes sideways, I need you to move. Fast."

Hayden nodded, eyes never leaving Marcel. "You go dark too long, we're coming in. Plan or no plan."

Before he could say more, Nyomi's rental truck pulled up next to them, with Nate behind the wheel. Nate stepped out, arms crossed, frustration mixed with a hint of respect in his stare.

"So this inside job of yours ; what's the move?"

Marcel's face was all grim determination.

"Meeting the recruiter from the flyer. He's my in to their operations."

Nate's brow creased.

"And we're just supposed to wait around?"

"More than that. Once I'm in, I'll feed you intel. Stay close, stay mobile. When I find out where they got Journey, if she's even there..."

Marcel trailed off, but his meaning was sharp. They all knew the odds.

"When I find her, we strike."

Nate looked at him.

"Feels like a setup, Marcel. Like you're walkin' blind into their trap."

Marcel smirked, a dark glint in his eye.

"Of course it's a trap. But we don't got a choice. From the outside, we're nothing. Only way to tear them down is to get inside and blow it up from there."

Nate exhaled.

"You get in too deep, we're not leaving you behind."

Marcel gave him a steady look.

"Don't worry about me. Worry about Journey."

Hayden cut in, glancing between them both.

"So we just play guard dogs, waiting for the whistle?"

"Stay sharp, stay close, be ready to move when I give the word."

Marcel's voice was a cold command, no room for anything else.

Nate stared at the ground for a second, rubbing his neck.

"We lose contact, we're coming in. I don't care if we blow the whole thing open."

Marcel nodded.

"That's why I need you both ready to make noise if it comes to that."

As they turned to look at the gas station, Hayden's gut twisted seeing the recruiter's car.

"And if this guy's as deadly as the others?"

"I'll deal with him," Marcel said, stepping out, checking his burner. "You two just be ready. We get Journey, we're burning this whole network to the ground."

Hayden's eyes followed Marcel as he crossed the lot.

"You better walk back out of this," he muttered.

Marcel paused, glancing back, a small grin showing.

"Looking too clean would get me killed. I'm just another guy looking for cash."

Hayden clenched his jaw, uneasy but trusting.

Marcel's figure grew smaller as he neared the recruiter's car, the weight of the mission heavy on all of them. Yet Marcel moved with a focus that spoke of a man who knew exactly what he was here to do, and exactly what it would cost.

63

The cold concrete walls of Sloan's stronghold felt like a tomb, locking Marcel and the other captives in a restless limbo. The air hung thick with tension, distant footsteps echoing through the narrow halls like a drumbeat counting down to their fate. Marcel had been in tight spots before, but this one held a different weight. Sloan was ruthless, and his henchmen, Trevor and Gus, weren't the type to show mercy.

Days slipped by, but Marcel began piecing together the fragments of conversation he overheard. Despite the coded talk, he knew enough. Trevor, the shotgun rider from his capture, wasn't just a grunt; he was one of Sloan's trusted enforcers. And Gus, the driver, played chess while others were playing checkers. Marcel caught glimpses of their strategy—Sloan and his lover, Lulu, were at odds, and Gus had played a critical role in setting up Lulu's brother. It was a house divided, and Marcel knew that kind of weakness was a way out.

Trevor, whether out of boredom or a grudging respect, started to talk more openly around Marcel. Marcel saw an opening. He knew Trevor was sick of the killing; he'd over-heard him on the phone one night, talking in code Marcel quickly deciphered. Trevor hated the blood on his hands, especially from murders ordered by Sloan and Lulu. Sloan's threats were lethal, trapping Trevor in a role that had slowly corroded his soul.

One night, after rounds of harsh drinks and card games between the guards, Marcel seized his chance.

"You know," Marcel began quietly, his voice low but firm enough to catch Trevor's ear, "this whole thing with Sloan and Lulu... it's coming down. You see it."

Trevor's jaw tightened, eyes fixed on the grimy floor as he tossed a deck of worn cards between his hands.

"You think you know how this plays out, huh? You're just a captive like the rest."

"Yeah, but I've been around men like Sloan. Men who think power is all about leashes. It doesn't last."

Marcel leaned in closer, voice dropping even lower. "If you're smart, and I think you are, you've got a backup plan. You already know what happens when that leash snaps, Trevor."

Long silence. The hum of electricity filled the space between them. Trevor's hands stilled on the cards before he finally met Marcel's eyes, a flicker of recognition passing between them.

"What are you getting at?"

Marcel didn't flinch.

"I've got someone on the outside. We could all get out of here, but I need your help to make the call."

Trevor's brow furrowed, his face skeptical but touched with something else; hope or desperation.

"Who's this someone?"

"A resourceful guy," Marcel said, purposely not

mentioning Hayden. "Get a signal to him, and he'll find a way to get us out. All we need is the right moment."

Trevor's eyes shifted to the locked steel door, then back at Marcel.

"You're playing a dangerous game."

"I've got nothing left to lose," Marcel said simply. "But you? You've still got a way out. Help me make that call, and we all make it out of here and get paid too."

Trevor didn't respond right away. He stood, shoving the cards into his back pocket.

"Wait here," he muttered, slipping through a side door and leaving Marcel with his heart pounding.

...

Hours later, Trevor returned, pulling Marcel aside into a quiet corner of the room.

"I've got a burner phone. If Sloan catches wind of this, we're both dead. Better be sure about your man on the other end."

Marcel nodded.

"Trust me, this guy is good. He'll come through."

Trevor passed the phone, and Marcel quickly dialed Hayden's number. It rang, and finally, a familiar voice crackled through the speaker.

"Marcel?"

Hayden's voice was thick with concern.

"Yeah, it's me," Marcel breathed out, relief flooding him. "It's bad. Sloan's got me locked in one of his strongholds, but I've made contact with some of his guys; there's a way out, but we'll need you."

"Where are you?" Hayden asked, his tone shifting, sharpening.

"Don't know the exact spot," Marcel admitted, "sending coordinates. Get Nate and Nyomi. We need everyone, dogs included."

A pause, then Hayden came back, clear and sharp.

"We're on it. Nate, Nyomi, and the dogs are prepped. What else?"

Marcel glanced at Trevor hovering nearby, his face tense.

"We need a distraction big enough to pull Sloan's attention off us."

Hayden hesitated only a moment.

"I've got a few tricks. We'll make it happen. Just be ready."

"I'll be ready," Marcel promised.

Trevor shifted uneasily.

"We won't get many chances."

"I know," Marcel said, pocketing the burner. "But it's better than waiting to get buried under Sloan's thumb."

...

Back at Buddy's friend Raymond's remote cabin, Hayden turned the call over to Nate and Nyomi gripped Beam, who was pacing restlessly, while Houston lay at his feet, ears alert.

"So, what's the plan?" Nate's voice was tight.

Hayden rubbed his temple.

"Marcel needs a big distraction to throw Sloan off. We have to hit them hard and fast."

Nyomi, always thinking ahead, frowned.

"Strike too soon, they'll lock down. Wait too long…"

"We hit tomorrow night," Hayden interrupted. "Quick and clean. Nate, get the dogs ready. Nyomi, go get Nate's brother and his lady friend. Nate has the address."

Nyomi nodded, determination sharp in her eyes, hope for Journey's rescue undimmed.

"We'll be ready."

Hayden turned back to the map sprawled across the table, fingers tracing possible routes. Thoughts of Marcel behind enemy lines clouded his mind, but he knew one thing for sure—Marcel was a strategist who'd tear Sloan's empire apart, brick by brick.

...

In the dim light of the stronghold, Marcel locked eyes with Trevor.

"It's on tomorrow night. You with me?"

Trevor's expression hardened, but he nodded. Tomorrow, they'd be free—or die trying.

64

Trevor's boots cut through the silence, the dull thud against the bunker's concrete floor. His fingers twitched near the holstered gun, eyes sweeping every corner, every darkened stretch, but his mind was somewhere else. The weight of the life he'd carved out for himself hung heavy on his shoulders. Nights spent in blood-soaked silence, the faces of men who would never breathe again, their empty stares haunting him. Those faces pulled at his soul, a constant reminder of the depths he'd plunged into Sloan's world.

His jaw tightened, his pace slowing as he approached the storage room. Doubt cut through him like a knife, sharp and relentless. Crossing Sloan, living to see the other side of that choice, felt like a suicide wish. But the hatred seething in his chest was fierce enough to drown out the fear. Sloan's smug sneers, the way he tossed people aside like trash, the endless games. Trevor felt it deep, like a sickness twisting in his gut.

He paused, leaning his back against the wall, the cold concrete pressing through his clothes. This was it. No turning back. Memories tore through him, the first man he'd gunned down, his face frozen in shock; the last one, pleading, voice breaking. Trevor's stomach twisted. Enough was enough. He couldn't do this anymore.

His grip tightened around the gun, his breath shaky as he steeled himself. If Marcel failed, if everything went to hell, Trevor would disappear. No one knew his connection to Marcel. Sloan had no clue, none of them did. But Trevor knew, and that was enough. That knowledge was a poison, eating at him from the inside, leaving nothing but ashes.

65

The Nevada heat hit like a sledgehammer that morning, smothering the air with a dry, unyielding heaviness that promised a blistering day. Raymond's safe house sat low and quiet; a modest, weather-beaten structure hidden in the emptiness off Route Fifty. Inside, the place felt just as worn, with mismatched chairs and old leather couches that had seen better years. Dust lingered thick in the air, adding to the weight of silence hanging over them. Faded wallpaper peeled from the walls, the edges curling like a quiet surrender. In one corner, stacks of newspapers piled up, alongside a table cluttered with scattered papers and cigars.

As Hayden, Nate, and Nyomi waited, Nyomi wandered off into a back room. Amidst boxes stacked high and low, she stumbled on a cluster of old photographs, yellowed with age and time. One caught her eye—a snapshot of Buddy, Raymond, and Marcel. Marcel couldn't have been older than fourteen, but his eyes had that look, fierce, intense, like he'd already seen things that hardened him. Lean but fierce, a kid who'd already shed too much innocence. Buddy and Raymond stood beside him, both strong, faces hard, like they were already grooming Marcel for something far beyond what anyone should've been ready for at that age. Nyomi felt the weight of it, a chill settling in her gut.

The burner phone buzzed in Hayden's pocket, vibrating like a warning in the thick silence. He glanced down, fingers tense as he picked it up. The voice on the other end came through low and rough, unmistakable.

"It's Trevor," the man said, voice clipped. "I got something for you. Marcel's got a plan."

Hayden stepped outside, letting the desert air hit him hard as he put distance between himself and the others.

"Go ahead," he said, keeping his tone steady, though he could feel the tension winding tight in his chest.

Trevor's voice came through again, quieter now, but sharp.

"Guards switch every four hours. Slack comes in right around shift change. You've got a ten-minute window when security's light. Marcel's already scoped it. He'll make his move then."

Hayden nodded, already mapping it out in his head.

"And the layout?"

"There's a back corridor that leads to a service exit, past the barracks. Lightly guarded, since it's mostly used for maintenance. Marcel's going out that way. Once he's out, he'll head north. You need to park off the main road, about half a mile out. There's a rock formation big enough to hide a car. Park there and wait."

Hayden's gaze drifted to the horizon, scanning it as his mind turned the plan over. The risk sat heavy on his shoulders, but he pushed through the doubt.

Trevor exhaled, a worn-out sound that echoed the weight of the whole situation.

"Look, man, don't matter if you trust me. Marcel's counting on this. I got no reason to set him up, and neither do you."

A silence hung between them, thick and loaded.

"No one else knows?" Hayden's voice came out even, steel hidden beneath the calm.

"No one but me," Trevor replied. "If this thing blows, I'm the one they'll pin it on. Marcel's kept you out clean. Just know you've got the better end here."

Hayden's grip tightened around the phone.

"Alright. I'll be there. Don't mess this up."

Trevor's voice came back softer, almost ghostly.

"I won't."

Then the line went dead.

Hayden stood still for a moment, staring out into the relentless heat, the weight of what was about to happen settling heavy in his gut. It was time.

66

The desert night was closing in, sky shifting from a blistering orange to deep purple. Hayden stood beside Nate, both washed in the dim glow of a single lantern hanging from a post outside Raymond's safe house. The air was thick with tension as they loaded up, the ground around them scattered with rifles, handguns, boxes of ammo spread out like offerings for a battle nobody would walk away from unchanged.

Hayden wiped sweat from his brow, checked his phone again. Marcel was still in that bunker, depending on them to be ready when it counted. Time dragged slow, each minute stretching out, pressure mounting. The margin for error was thin as paper.

"Think we got enough firepower?" Nate's voice was low as he shoved another box of ammo into the truck bed, a mix of nerves and determination in his eyes.

Hayden nodded.

"More than enough. Just gotta hit fast and hit hard. We don't get to fuck this up."

The plan was set. Marcel had slipped them the details

he'd gathered from the inside. That intel came through Trevor, a turncoat from Sloan's own camp, playing both sides, though Hayden felt the weight of distrust every time he thought of Trevor. But that wasn't their problem tonight. They had what they needed—layout, guard shifts, and the spot where Marcel would make his move. It was now or never.

"Raymond's truck is ready to roll," Nate said, securing the last box.

"We get in, pull Marcel and the others out, and vanish before they even know what hit them."

Hayden's mind was already deep in the raid, plotting every step. It had to be sharp, clean. Marcel's intel was solid —he'd mapped the security, pinpointed weak spots, and most importantly, the back way out. They'd be ghosts, gone before Sloan's men knew their empire was burning. Hayden loaded the last weapon, glanced at Nate.

"We go in at midnight. Not a minute off. Everyone better be ready."

Nate nodded.

"You got it."

As Hayden climbed into the driver's seat, his mind turned dark with focus. Marcel was waiting out there, every second slipping away. The weight of it all pressed heavy. Failure was not an option.

...

Sloan sat at the head of a long mahogany table, fingers drumming softly on polished wood. Around him, his business associates relaxed, nursing glasses of high-end whiskey. His top men, stone-faced and strapped, stood like statues by the doors, eyes sharp, silent.

"Gentlemen," Sloan began, voice smooth but carrying an edge of control. "We've had a good run. Expansion is inevitable—more clients, more product, more territory." He leaned back, a grin spreading. "Best part? No one's on to us. This city will be ours."

One businessman, a thickset man with thinning hair, swirled his glass, nodding.

"The cops are covered?"

Sloan chuckled, smug.

"Paid and smiling. They'll look the other way long as the money keeps flowing. Got the chief himself on the hook. We're untouchable."

Another associate, lean and sharp-eyed, eyed Sloan with a flicker of doubt.

"And security? The bunker's tight?"

Sloan's expression stayed cool.

"Locked down. Guards know their place and what happens if they slip. We installed new surveillance last week. Nothing moves without me knowing."

The sharp-eyed man took a sip, eyes never leaving Sloan.

"What about loyalty? You trust your men?"

Sloan waved it off, confidence pouring from every gesture.

"They know who keeps them fed, who keeps them in the life. They do their jobs; we're golden."

A low hum of agreement rippled through the room, but Sloan's lieutenants stayed stone-faced, eyes fixed forward, unreadable. One of them, a burly man with a scar running down his cheek, shifted but stayed silent.

Sloan leaned in, his grin sharp as a blade.

"Listen up. We're going global. Dario's got the Mexico

connection lined up. Product's crossing borders soon. We're untouchable."

His associates nodded, buying into the empire's promise. But while Sloan sat there, chest puffed up with pride, he missed the fractures snaking through his empire, blind to the storm building right under him.

67

The bunker reeked of dampness; mildew laced with cheap cologne. As Marcel moved deeper into the compound, that stench clung to him, marking every step he took into the beast's belly. The walls seemed to press in tighter, and the air thickened with a buzz of sinister activity.

Marcel kept his head down, playing the role. He was stuck doing grunt work, lugging supplies from one end of the bunker to the other. Boxes stacked with food, drugs, maybe even weapons. Each time he passed a guard, they barely glanced at him, just grunted or nodded. His cover was intact, but he knew he couldn't slip.

Rounding a corner, Marcel spotted something—a couple of figures in a bright room, voices low but sharp. He recognized one of them: Gus. Same man who picked him up, voice rough, eyes dead and hollow. But the other man, he was something different. Clean-cut suit, too sharp for this grimy shithole. This one was definitely a higher up.

Their conversation was muffled, but Marcel caught bits.

"...shipment delayed...Los Angeles...extra girls and boys...more eyes on us."

Marcel's gut twisted. Could one of them be Journey? He lingered a little longer, adjusting his grip on the box, straining to catch more.

"...next round is the big one...Journey's already in place..."

His heart froze. Journey. She was here. Alive. Every nerve in his body screamed to charge in, grab that man by his collar, and demand answers. But he couldn't do it. Not yet. He needed leverage, intel, and something concrete.

Drawing a breath, Marcel reined in the adrenaline threatening to blow his cover. He continued down the hall, grip steady on the box, acting like he hadn't heard a thing. But his mind was on fire.

...

Hayden sat in the car, fidgeting. Waiting grated on him. The Nevada desert stretched out in all directions, endless, desolate, but his eyes were locked on the bunker in the distance. Each minute felt like an hour. He glanced at Nate, half-reclined, eyes hooded but sharp. Nyomi and the dogs were stashed in the other vehicle, all ready, just waiting on Marcel's call.

"He's taking too long," Hayden muttered. His leg bounced, nerves edgy. "We should've been closer."

Nate cracked one eye open, giving him a look.

"He knows what he's doing."

Hayden gritted his teeth. His hand hovered near his phone, waiting for that signal. He trusted Marcel, but that didn't ease the gnawing feeling in his gut. Marcel was in there, alone, while they sat out here, powerless.

"If he needs us, he'll call," Nate said, his voice calm but tight. He felt it too, that coiled tension beneath the calm. They both did.

But for now, all they could do was wait.

...

The hallway ended at a heavy steel door, one that needed a keycard Marcel didn't have. He'd noticed it in the security setup earlier—restricted access, probably where the girls were kept. If Journey was here, she'd be behind that door.

He set the box down, pretending to check something in his pocket. A guard passed by, swiped his card, and the door clicked open. Marcel took in the motion from the corner of his eye, noting the sequence. When the door swung shut behind the guard, he edged closer, running through his options.

Strike now? Force the door, slip inside, maybe find Journey, get her out. But it was risky. Too risky. He had no idea how many guards were inside, and with Gus in the mix, he knew this was bigger than he could handle solo.

He needed more time. Needed to scope the place, learn the layout, clock the guards' shifts. Most of all, he needed proof Journey was here, that she was alive and close enough to grab.

His hand balled into a fist. Every part of him screamed to act, but his mind held cold and clear. Blowing this now wasn't an option. Not when he'd come so far.

He backed away from the door, noting every detail. He'd be back. But first, he had to get word to Hayden, let them know he was closing in. He knew they were outside, waiting, patience stretched thin.

The burner phone Trevor handed him buzzed in his pocket. He pulled it out, keeping it low.

A single message: "Where the hell are you?"

It was Hayden.

Marcel smirked, slipping the phone back into his pocket. Soon. Just a little more time.

But even as he told himself that, he knew one thing—things were about to get ugly.

68

The knock at the door was barely audible, but in the silence, it felt like thunder. Floyd and Katia exchanged tense looks, both knowing they couldn't stay still for long. Katia, seated on the edge of the bed, gripped the small gun she'd swiped off the cut down goons last week. Her knuckles were white, eyes like steel. Floyd signaled for her to stay low, stepping toward the door in silence.

The old carpet muffled his steps as he got closer, heart racing but hand steady on his gun. Nate had said they'd send someone, but trust didn't come easy. He took a slow breath, looked through the peephole, and saw a woman standing there—had to be Nyomi. He loosened his grip just a bit, still cautious. With precise moves, he unlocked the door, cracked it open, gun still ready.

Nyomi stood there, eyes sharp but calm, recognizing him just as he recognized her. He opened the door a little wider, just enough to let her in, but the tension held strong.

"We need to move," Nyomi said, her voice quiet but firm.

Floyd nodded, motioning for Katia to follow. Relief flashed across Katia's face, quick but real.

...

They piled into the jeep, silence hanging heavy as Nyomi took the wheel. Floyd sat in the passenger seat, eyes scanning the streets, while Katia was quiet in the back. Only the hum of the engine broke the stillness as Nyomi steered through the empty outskirts.

Minutes passed before Nyomi spoke, glancing at Floyd.

"How'd you two get together? Last I heard, Katia was missing for years, and you... Nate didn't even know if you were alive."

Floyd kept his eyes forward, voice low.

"Been underground a long time... literally. Bunker life. No idea what was going on outside, just trying to survive day by day. When I fought my way out, I found Katia." He paused, looking back at her. "We swore to get up out of here together."

Nyomi's gaze flicked to the rearview mirror, catching Katia's eyes. She sat there, hands clasped, looking like she was somewhere else. Nyomi's question hung in the air, unspoken but felt. "Katia... remember anything? Anything about Journey? She's my daughter."

Katia's eyes snapped to the mirror, unreadable. She was quiet, like she was deciding how much to share. Finally, her voice came, low but steady. "Journey... I heard that name a few times. Too many girls to remember clear. If she's still around, she's in deep. They don't just let you go."

Nyomi's grip tightened on the wheel.

"Know where they might have her? Any places they kept you?"

Katia exhaled, her fists clenched.

"They moved us a lot. But there was one place... they called it 'The Haven.'" The irony cut through her voice. "It was no haven, not for us. If she's anywhere, it's probably there."

Nyomi's jaw set, her mind racing.

"Someone who knows where this place is?"

Katia shook her head.

"Not exactly. They blindfolded us every time. But there's someone close to Sloan who might know. One of his favorites. We'd need to find her without tipping anyone off."

Nyomi's eyes met Floyd's, both knowing what that meant.

"Think she could lead us to Journey?" Nyomi's voice was solid, unwavering, as she looked back at Floyd.

"Maybe. But we're putting her life at risk, Nyomi," Floyd said.

The jeep rolled through a deserted intersection. This was about more than getting answers now; it was a race against time. Nyomi looked back at Katia.

"Appreciate you telling me. We're finding her. Sloan and his people don't get to win."

Katia stared down at her hands.

"Hope you're right."

The silence returned, heavy but determined. At least now they had a lead.

Then, out of nowhere, Nyomi caught sight of headlights speeding up behind them. They were coming in too fast.

"Get ready," Floyd muttered, hand on his gun. The dark sedan behind them crashed into the jeep, metal crunching as they spiraled out of control.

The world flipped, metal screeching, glass shattering, a blur of pain and chaos.

...

The sedan hit hard from the side, sending the jeep skidding and spinning. It flipped, rolled, end over end, until it finally came to a brutal halt, upside down, nearly five hundred yards from the hit.

Nyomi's ears pounded as she hung upside down in the seat. She unbuckled, twisted out, the pain sharp, but she kept moving. Floyd groaned nearby but was still with her. So was Katia, but they weren't alone.

Through the cracked windshield, Katia recognized him—one of Sloan's muscle, no doubt. A hulking brute with a face scarred in a sneer that never left. Dark hair slicked back, tattoos crawling up muscled arms, silver tooth flashing. He stepped out with his gun drawn, closing in on them like he owned the place.

No time to think. Nyomi grabbed her gun and fired. One shot, sharp in the night air.

Pure instinct or luck, it didn't matter. The bullet hit dead center, dropping him where he stood. Eyes wide in shock before he hit the pavement, lifeless.

Floyd, shaky but unhurt, crawled out of the wreckage, eyes on the body.

"We gotta move. Now."

Nyomi nodded, but Floyd had one more thing in mind. He crouched next to the goon's body, found the man's phone. Locked, just as he thought. They'd need the goon's thumb to open it. He pulled out his knife, slicing off the thumb without a second thought, pocketing it.

"Let's go.

The three of them disappeared into the night, leaving the wreckage behind.

69

arcel lay sprawled on the cold, damp floor, clutching his stomach as Sloan's brute squad closed in around him. His face twisted in pain, and he groaned, curling into himself. Their laughter echoed in the room as one of them landed a solid kick to his ribs, rolling him onto his back. This was part of Marcel's plan; to catch some blows. Buddy taught Marcel this by the time he was eleven.

"Look at this tough guy now," one goon sneered, spitting beside Marcel. Another stepped forward, taking his time, savoring the moment as he stomped down on Marcel's shoulder. Marcel let out a grunt, and the trafficked captives looked on, their glimmers of hope dimming with each blow Marcel took.

"You're nothing but talk, huh?" the trafficker hissed, swinging his boot toward Marcel's face. Marcel flinched, letting the kick just skim his head. The trafficking goons laughed, their guard down, fully enjoying their moment. Marcel stayed down, his breathing shallow, his movements slow, almost shaking. One of the bigger enforcers grinned, showing yellowed, menacing teeth as he stepped in, ready to finish Marcel off. He raised his foot high, aiming for Marcel's chest. Just before it came down, Marcel's eyes flared, and his body sprang into action.

In one swift motion, Marcel grabbed the enforcer's ankle, twisting it with brutal force. A snap echoed as the man screamed, collapsing to the floor. The rest of the goons fell back, caught off guard, but Marcel was already on his feet, moving with deadly purpose. One of them swung a fist, but Marcel dodged, countering with a sharp elbow to the throat, then a kick to the knee, dropping him. Spinning around, he caught another's knife strike, twisting the man's wrist until it broke. A captive let out a scream, not from fear, but rallying. This wasn't just a distraction anymore; it was an uprising.

The last enforcer charged from behind, wielding a pipe, but Marcel sidestepped, slamming his assailant's head into the wall. The pipe clattered to the ground, and in a flash, Marcel picked it up, swinging it with brutal speed. The dull thud of metal on bone filled the room, and Sloan's goons lay scattered, some unconscious, some lifeless. Marcel stood in the center, chest heaving, eyes cold and focused. The captives looked at him, fear replaced by something new-hope. They began moving, just as Marcel had planned, creating more chaos, throwing the remaining guards off balance. Marcel wiped a drop of blood from his mouth, looking over the freed captives.

"Now," he said, his voice low, "we finish this."

The captives spread out through the warehouse, moving fast and silent. Marcel stayed stone-faced as he surveyed the scene. Bodies of Sloan's enforcers lay scattered, but there was one last piece of business to handle. Hayden dragged a guard forward, trembling as he pressed a gun against the back of the man's head. The cold steel had the man spilling his guts, every word coming out in fear.

"L-Lulu's address ... outskirts near Ridgewood. The whole operations there. I swear, that's everything. Please, I told you everything!"

The man whimpered, his hands shaking, desperate.

Marcel crouched, studying him with those cold, unreadable eyes. Without a word, he reached into his jacket and pulled out his Glock. The guard's face twisted in terror, realizing he was out of options.

"You did."

Marcel rose and, with one swift motion, shot the guard in the leg. The man screamed, clutching his knee as blood poured out. Marcel stayed calm, detached. He raised his gun again, this time firing straight into the back of the man's head. The guard's body dropped, lifeless. Nate, who'd found car keys on the dead guards, didn't even flinch, but the captives took in the scene with a new under-standing of what Marcel had just done for them.

Hayden glanced down at the corpse, then at Marcel, who holstered his weapon without a second look. Marcel turned to the captives, his expression hardening.

"We'll use Sloan and Lulu's little rift, but right now, focus is on Sloan. From what I gathered, he's got something up his sleeve, so let's keep moving. Don't get stupid, don't get reckless. This fucking tyrant's reign ends tonight."

Nate handed keys to those ready to drive, and one by one, the captives piled into the vehicles once owned by Sloan. They disappeared into the night, ready for whatever lay ahead. Once Nate was moving, Nyomi called Hayden, telling him she was with Floyd and Katia, but they were on foot. Time was tight.

70

Lulu's mini-mansion stood like a lone sentinel in the barren Nevada desert, a testament to the secrecy that wrapped her life. From the outside, it looked sleek but low-key, designed to blend into the rugged landscape with sand-colored stucco walls, broad, tinted windows hiding the world within, and a roof that hugged low to the ground. Inside, the luxury was cold, almost surgical—marble floors, minimalist furnishings, a sharp elegance that felt as out of place as it was meticulously placed. Abstract art hung on the walls, each piece as detached and cryptic as the woman who chose them. Tension clung to the air, silent but thick, a direct contrast to the heat and chaos spilling over from her illicit world.

The desert around her was relentless, stretching out like an endless stage for something grim and unforgiving. Pale scrub brush dotted the red sands, and the wind carried a constant low howl. Jagged mountains loomed in the distance, baking under the relentless sun, while any sign of life or civilization was long out of sight. Henderson was the nearest city, with its neon-lit casinos, the pull of tourists, and streams of cash. But out here, it was another world entirely—isolated, desolate, and perfect for a woman like Lulu to do her work undisturbed.

Inside, Lulu was caught up in the moment, living out a scene of dominance and lust. Trevor's body towered over her, his motions rhythmically commanding, while Candice, Sloan's once favorite and Katia's ex-roommate, followed Lulu's exact orders. Her mouth traced along Lulu's body, precise, like every touch was scripted for power and satisfaction.

The mood shattered with the ring of her phone. Marcel's voice came through, steady but direct, delivering words that split her reality apart. Sloan had killed Richard. The news hit her like a bullet. Her whole body tensed, rage burning hot and fast. She barely paused before giving Marcel Sloan's precise location, her mind already spinning out the vengeance she was planning. As the call ended, a dark fire flickered in her eyes. She was set on a single mission.

"Get the fuck out," she barked, her voice sharp, final.

Trevor didn't hesitate, his body jolting as he scrambled out of the room, his footsteps a rapid beat on the floor, heading to the car. Candice, slower, sensed something in the air, dark and boiling, though she didn't fully understand it. Trevor reached for the car door, his fingers grazing the handle—oblivious to the C4 wired up to every inch of the mini-mansion.

The explosion came in one violent sweep, the C4 detonating with a roar that swallowed the entire house in flames. The blast ripped through everything, engulfing Lulu, Candice, and Trevor in a blaze that left no mercy. Shards of debris rained down, ash and fire billowing into the desert sky, erasing everything and everyone.

Sloan's plan played out perfectly, unwittingly feeding into Marcel's larger scheme. With Lulu gone, Sloan's empire was slipping, falling piece by piece, and he didn't even realize how close Marcel was, watching, waiting to strike. Marcel hadn't expected it to fall so quickly, but letting Sloan's paranoia clear the path only made his job easier. Trevor's death was just a bonus, a loose end tied up without Marcel lifting a finger. Mistakes had no place here, especially any potential threat that was eliminated in one clean sweep.

71

As the morning sun climbed over the horizon, Hayden and Marcel gathered the freed captives outside the safe-house. Some had already slipped into the night, but most stayed, lost, with nowhere else to turn. While they laid down instructions, Nyomi hung back, her gaze steady on Nate and Floyd. First time the brothers had seen each other since Floyd got tangled up in that life, sold like property. Floyd's face showed the wear, but his mind stayed sharp, and the second he asked about their mother, Nate's eyes betrayed the truth he'd tried to bury.

Before hitting Milwaukee, Marcel had given Nate a hard warning: keep their mother's death locked down until the time was right. Didn't want Floyd's head clouded with grief. But Floyd saw right through him. The truth was written all over Nate's face, and just like that, the weight of his mother's passing crushed down on him. A fire burned in Floyd's chest, hotter than anything he'd felt since being trapped in the dark. Couldn't tell her he loved her one last time, but he could still make the ones responsible bleed for it.

After that heavy reunion, Marcel spoke up, looking every one of them dead in the eye.

"Get some rest while you can. Death could come for us any second, but we're not running. Reprisal is coming."

The captives nodded in silence, no flinching, every one of them ready to see it through.

...

Over at a high-end spot on the Vegas Strip, Sloan paced in tight circles, voice snarling through the speakerphone. Orders flew like bullets.

"I need more men. Floyd and Katia are out there, and I'm not losing another dollar because of this bullshit!"

In the corner, Journey sank deeper into herself, the words whipping past like razors. He'd owned her for too long, and her spirit was a hollow shell, worn down and discarded. Other women at the farm got passed around, used, but he held her back, waiting, watching. Ever since his eyes landed on her, she'd been his. With Lulu's ashes blown somewhere into the desert, he figured it was his chance now. He'd make her his main woman, mold her into what he wanted, protect her from the scraps and the gutter, shield her from anything that dared oppose him despite her age.

The phone call shifted, a darker tone creeping in as one of his goons reported from the bunker.

"A lot dead, broken security, captives gone. What's next?"

Sloan's jaw flexed, eyes cold with a calculating gleam.

"Head to the Haven," Sloan shouted, voice like a blade.

"We'll regroup there. No one's touching us while we set things straight!"

The "Haven" was Sloan's fortress, a place buried miles deep into nowhere. From the outside, it looked like any backcountry ranch, isolated, locked away from prying eyes. But it held a nightmare underground, a dungeon for women, trafficked, brutalized, treated like flesh on a conveyor. Those who survived were little more than ghosts, moving in silence, fear tying their souls down.

Journey was held there too, claimed and kept close by Sloan's eye. He watched her like a wolf on a deer, waiting for that moment when he'd break her for good. Peace was a word she barely remembered, every day dragging her closer to the edge of nothing. But deep down, some small piece of her still clung to one final thread of hope, that maybe this life would end, one way or another.

72

The guard sat slack, lost in the glow of his phone, eyes glued to explicit photos. A lazy smirk spread across his face, fingers flicking through images while the car's warmth pulled him into a daze. His window was halfway down, but he didn't hear the crunch of gravel behind him, didn't see the shadow slipping closer. Marcel moved like a ghost in the darkness, every step calculated, expression stone-cold. In one swift motion, his hand clamped around the guard's jaw, yanking his head back with a single, sickening crack. The guard's phone tumbled from his fingers as his body went limp. Marcel lowered the corpse carefully onto the seat, making sure not a sound would reach any other ears.

He didn't pause; his next target was already in motion. Another guard was circling the perimeter, eyes scanning the compound. Something felt off. The hairs on his neck prickled as he spotted the slumped figure in the car. He cursed under his breath and pulled out his radio, tension turning his voice sharp.

"We got a breach. One of ours is down. Everyone, strap up. It's go-time."

Inside the main building, Sloan and his top men, Gus and a handful of others, were deep in conversation, the air thick with frustration. Niko had been bested by Floyd's crew, and they were feeling the sting. Gus shook his head.

"How did Niko let that happen," Gus growled.

Sloan's face twisted.

"Doesn't matter now. We got bigger problems."

Before Sloan could lay out his plan, a guard burst in.

"Sloan! We got a breach. Locals storming in! One of ours is dead!"

Sloan's face darkened.

"Everyone, get ready. We're taking these motherfuckers down!" Sloan yelled.

His men moved quick, hands flashing over guns, loading them like they'd done a thousand times. They were ready for war. Outside, Marcel's team was already facing fire. Sloan's elite guards moved with deadly precision, bullets flying, each shot meant to kill. Marcel's crew pushed forward, struggling to hold their ground. A bullet grazed Marcel's ribs, while Hayden stumbled, a bullet tearing into his shoulder. Floyd took a hit-his body crumpled, blood pooling beneath him as he clung to life.

Nate saw his brother fall, and something snapped. A roar ripped from his chest as he fired wild, taking down two advancing guards. His eyes burned with rage, moving with a fury that could only come from loss, from a thirst for revenge. But the chaos kept coming. Out of the shadows emerged men and women, brainwashed by Sloan, their faces blank, their hands gripping guns like they'd been trained to obey without a thought. They opened fire, their aim dead-on, as if programmed for this.

Marcel knew what had to be done. He flipped the switch on his Glock 48. The gun spit bullets in rapid bursts, cutting down the brainwashed attackers one by one until the field was clear of bodies.

But the real fight waited.

Marcel led the charge, mind sharp despite the sting in his side. Hayden followed close, with Amara, a fierce, strikingly beautiful woman who'd survived the carnage, at their heels. Her mahogany skin glowed against the backdrop of blood and dirt, her dark waves of hair framing her almond-shaped eyes sharp with focus. She was no longer a captive now; with a gun in her hand, she was a warrior.

They found Sloan in the last room of the Haven. Marcel kicked open the door, eyes zeroing in on Sloan, who had Journey trapped in front of him, arm tight around her neck, a gun pressed to her head. Journey's eyes were wide, her half-naked body shaking, her skin prickling with cold and fear. Sloan smirked, smug, like he held all the cards.

"One wrong move and her brains will stain these walls!"

Marcel let his gun drop to the floor, one hand raising slower than the other, his face unreadable. His fingers twitched before reaching for the knife, brushing against the cold steel. Instead of grabbing the handle outright, he pinched the flat of the blade between his fingers, careful and deliberate. With a slow, practiced motion, he let the weight of the handle tip forward into his palm, shifting it into a firm grip.

"You win, Sloan," he said, voice cold.

Before Sloan could react, Marcel's arm flicked forward. The knife flew, embedding itself deep in Sloan's eye. The man staggered back, his grip on Journey loosening, mouth open in a silent scream. He hit the ground hard, the blade burying deeper into his skull. Sloan's reign ended there-his brain just as dead as his black heart. Marcel moved to Journey's side, grabbing a blanket from a chair and wrapping it around her shivering shoulders.

"You're safe now," he said.

Amara and Hayden dashed outside to find Floyd, urgency driving them forward. The sun was rising over the blood-soaked Haven, casting a cold light on the chaos they were leaving behind. The reign of terror Sloan had built was over, finally finished.

73

Evan Greene, a light-skinned Black man pushing sixty-five, wore years of life in the creases of his peppered face, his five o'clock shadow just as weathered. His hands, though, still steady as stone, like back when he was in the OR with a scalpel in hand. Reasons for why he lost his license, still murky. Marcel gave him a nod. Evan was his godfather, but that didn't mean he was a stranger to patching up folks in need. Thirty years back, he'd kept Buddy breathing after four slugs tore him up, and that night bonded him, Buddy, and Raymond for life.

Without missing a beat, Evan had two loyal men load Floyd into a ride, the kind that wouldn't be followed. That bullet had come within an inch of taking Floyd's life. Blood loss was real, and Marcel could see Evan's concern in his eyes.

"A hair closer, Marcel, and we'd be talking about something else."

Marcel watched in silence as they drove away, knowing Floyd's only shot was with the man who'd once brought Buddy back from the brink. Nate watched the departing

Tahoe with his brother in it, clinging to life, his heart heavy with fear.

"I can't lose Floyd... not now," he whispered, almost to himself. Tears filled his eyes, and his hand trembled as he fought to hold himself together.

Marcel laid a gentle hand on his shoulder.

"He's strong. He'll make it."

...

Katia's hands trembled as she thought of the blood soaking through the fabric of Floyd's shirt. A hollow ache spread through her chest; Floyd saved her life. If she was going to be with a man after suffering this three year long sex trafficking ordeal, it would definitely be Floyd. Her trust in any other man was lost.

...

Marcel crouched next to Nyomi, brushing a hand over her shoulder. Her eyes flickered open, dazed, then sharpened as she remembered where she was. Reality hit her hard, and tears started to flow, her sobs tearing through the quiet.

"Mommy," Journey's voice broke, her own tears falling. She reached for her mother, arms tight around her like she'd lose her again if she let go.

"Journey... baby girl..." Nyomi rocked her daughter, tears of relief and sorrow mingling. They clung to each other, reunited after hellish events neither one could speak of just yet.

Marcel hung back, giving them a moment. But when he glanced away, he caught Nyomi's eyes on him. Her sobs quieted, and she looked at him, something new and deep in her gaze. Marcel shifted, uncomfortable. He was used to handling business, not this kind of tenderness.

Through her tears, Nyomi managed a smile, wiping her face.

"I had my doubts about you, Marcel. Men without jobs, no direction... I've seen that before. But you—you promised to bring my daughter back. And you did it. No excuses, no running around."

Marcel's head dropped shyly.

"Had to do what needed to be done," he muttered.

Nyomi chuckled, then leaned in, surprising him with a kiss. His eyes went wide, his heart kicking up. The warmth of it took him off guard, full of gratitude, maybe something else too. When she pulled back, Marcel was speechless.

Nyomi's voice softened.

"Marcel... I want you in our lives. I know it's sudden, but... I'm not ready to let you go."

Marcel hesitated, not from doubt but from truth.

"I live off the grid, Nyomi. Always been that way. I'm not even on the census. My Pops, Buddy, he taught me to keep moving, never settle. His ex in Nebraska home-schooled me, but life's never been normal."

She drew him into her arms, and Marcel found himself easing into her warmth. Their next kiss deepened, slow, leaving no need for words. It was all understood between them.

...

Hayden and Nate talked in low tones, a rare peace between them.

"I'm not built for the badge anymore," Hayden admitted. "That bigotry in the department, the way the blacks get looked at and treated. I can't be a part of that."

Nate nodded. "I get it, man. It messed you up. But look, you spoke out, and people saw that. They got it on record."

"Doesn't matter," Hayden sighed, weight in his voice. "Cybil's been saying she wanted me out anyway."

A small smile crossed Nate's face.

"She'll be glad to hear it, no doubt. Me, though... I want to help Marcel."

Marcel, catching the last of it, turned to Nate.

"Appreciate it, but I keep it low-key. Anything official's a risk. Buddy didn't exactly leave a clean trail behind us."

Nate grinned. "All good. I'll be the front man; you stay in the dark."

Marcel chuckled. "We'll see.

...

The room buzzed with a quiet conversation. Journey and Katia exchanged glances, something heavy sparking between them.

"You..." Katia's voice shook, the weight of exhaustion pressing down. "You knew him too, didn't you? Gerald... Curtis... Howard Lee?"

Journey tensed, her expression hardening.

"He went by Gerald with me."

"And he was Curtis when I met him," Katia replied, pain and anger sharpening her voice.

"Same man, same twisted game."

The connection between them, unspoken yet powerful, grew deeper—sisters forged by pain and survival. A tidal wave of realization hit them. They'd both been led into a nightmare by the same predator, reeled in through workshops run by Christina, the so-called saint of social work. Behind her mask of philanthropy, she was nothing but a trap, her web tangled with their worst memories.

Tears welled up, not just for the suffering they'd endured but for the fact they'd both survived. They didn't need words. They just held hands, leaning on each other in the silence, finding strength in the knowledge that the worst was behind them.

EPILOGUE

The applause bounced off the high ceilings of the grand ballroom, a wave of clapping hands and nodding heads, as the social worker grinned at the podium. Her polished smile was steady, eyes glinting under the bright lights as she held the award, fingers wrapped tight around the plaque engraved with her name. She looked like the picture of success, respectability-a pillar of the community. As she stepped down, moving through the crowd, she shook hands, exchanged pleasantries, the image of control. For a moment, she seemed untouchable. Her past, all her grime and secrets, sat hidden under layers of awards and empty promises. Then, a shift in the air.

"Excuse me, ma'am." A deep voice cut through.

She turned, smile slipping just a second, catching sight of two plainclothes officers, badges gleaming at their waists.

"What's this about?" Her voice dropped, face stiffening, though she already felt the fear creeping in. The taller officer moved closer, his eyes cold as steel.

"You're under arrest for your involvement in an organized human trafficking operation."

Her whole world shifted.

Hands grabbed her wrists, yanking them back. The smooth front cracked.

"Wait ... wait a minute!" She stammered, voice pitching. "You ... you've got it all wrong! I help people! I'm the one helping them!"

The officer started reading her rights, his voice a steady, unyielding tone.

"You have the right to remain silent. Anything you say can and will be used against you in a court of law ... "

Her heart slammed in her chest, the reality hitting her hard.

"This is a mistake! I was just trying to-"

"You have the right to an attorney. If you cannot afford one, one will be appointed to you ... "

The cuffs clicked, cold metal biting into her wrists. The room, once filled with applause, had turned dead silent. Eyes stared, whispers spread like wildfire, faces filled with disbelief. She could feel their gaze burning through her, each step with the officers feeling like she was dragging iron.

"I didn't do anything wrong!" she shouted, twisting against the cuffs. But it was too late. The mask was gone.

...

The dim prison lights flickered as Anthony Sykes, aka "Gerald" and "Curtis," lay in his cell, trapped in his own sweat and dread. Each echoing footstep down the concrete hall twisted his gut tighter. He knew his time was up and that it would be years before he hits the streets again.

Christina was already talking. And tonight, it came. The cell door creaked open, and there stood Benji, face cold as death, eyes locked on him. In his hand, a jagged, makeshift shank, sharpened and lethal. Anthony scrambled back, hands shaking.

"Benji, wait ... wait, we can talk about this, man!"

Benji's silence cut deeper than any words. The only sound was the scrape of the shank against the wall as he moved closer. Anthony's breath grew fast, sweat dripping cold down his neck. He was trapped. Helpless.

"Benji, please!" He choked out, voice breaking. "I didn't ... l didn't have a choice, you don't understand!"

But Benji's eyes held nothing but hatred, his jaw clenched, his body steady. Without a word, he lunged, driving the shank deep into Gerald's stomach.

The first stab was like fire tearing through him, a scream ripping from his throat. But Benji didn't stop. Again and again, the shank pierced flesh, drove through muscle, twisted in his gut, his chest, his sides. Gerald's screams bounced off the cell walls, his body thrashing as he tried to fight back, but his strength was fading, slipping with every vicious strike.

"P-please ... s-stop!" Gerald gasped, blood bubbling in his throat, his vision blurring, the taste of metal in his mouth.

Benji's face stayed blank, his hand relentless, every stab calculated, every thrust meant to break Gerald piece by piece. Blood splattered the walls, pooled thick beneath him as his body shuddered on the floor, nerves firing their last spasms of life. With one final plunge, Benji drove the shank deep into Gerald's chest, twisting it. Gerald's body jerked, his eyes stretched wide in terror, mouth open in a silent scream, the last of his breath escaping.

Benji stood over the corpse, chest heaving, the shank dripping blood in his grip. He looked down at the wreck he left behind, a raw, cold justice settling in him. Gerald lay lifeless, twisted and broken on the cold floor. It was done in the name of his cousin Katia, and all those young women he seduced into the sex trafficking ring. Benji wiped the shank on Gerald's jumpsuit, his face impassive. There was no remorse, no regret-only the raw satisfaction of knowing one more monster had met his end.

...

The sky hung low, an endless gray blanket stretched over Lakewood Park Beach, casting the water in soft, dull tones that seemed to hush the world around it. Early morning fog drifted lazily over the lake, clinging to the trees, resting like a shroud over the silent, still sand. Even the wind seemed to move in reverence, a gentle whisper over the glassy surface of the water, as if nature itself recognized the peace of the untouched dawn.

Sophia's bloated body floated near the shore, her lifeless form an unsettling addition to the quiet. Her eyes, once lit with ambition, now stared blankly into the murky depths beneath her, as if in silent communion with the secrets below. The soft lapping of the water against her limbs made a quiet rhythm, adding a peculiar serenity to the scene. The beach held its breath, the tranquility unbroken by human sound, undisturbed by the cares of the waking world.

But it was only a matter of time. Someone would see her, would spot her drifting there among the reeds. Her choice to follow greed over grace had led her here, to this unmarked grave in the lake's gentle grip. Instead of finding salvation in the Lord, she'd chased the promise of big money, quick and easy. Barry had her killed, tossed her into the lake like she was nothing more than a problem to be forgotten. Ever since the hit on Marcel had gone south, she knew too much, and that knowledge had cost her life.